IZNOGOUD

GOSCINNY - TABARY
THE WICKED WILES OF
IZNOGOUD

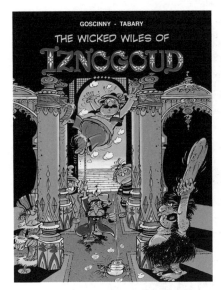

1 - THE WICKED WILES OF IZNOGOUD

GOSCINNY - TABARY
IZNOGOUD
THE CALIPH'S VACATION

2 - THE CALIPH'S VACATION

GOSCINNY - TABARY
IZNOGOUD
AND THE DAY OF MISRULE

3 - IZNOGOUD AND THE DAY OF MISRULE

COMING SOON

GOSCINNY - TABARY
IZNOGOUD
AND THE MAGIC COMPUTER

4 - IZNOGOUD AND THE MAGIC COMPUTER

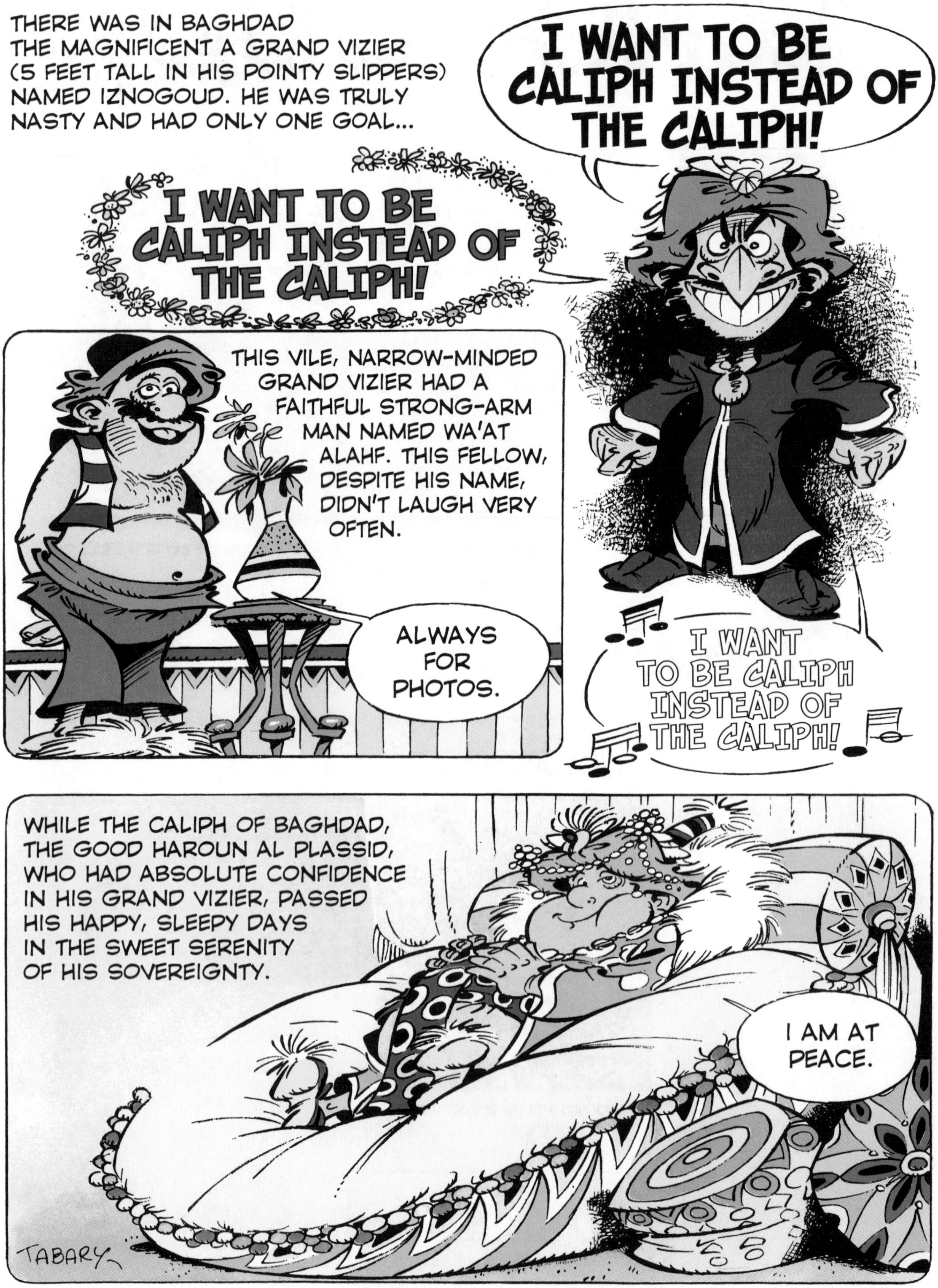
THERE WAS IN BAGHDAD THE MAGNIFICENT A GRAND VIZIER (5 FEET TALL IN HIS POINTY SLIPPERS) NAMED IZNOGOUD. HE WAS TRULY NASTY AND HAD ONLY ONE GOAL...
I WANT TO BE CALIPH INSTEAD OF THE CALIPH!
I WANT TO BE CALIPH INSTEAD OF THE CALIPH!
THIS VILE, NARROW-MINDED GRAND VIZIER HAD A FAITHFUL STRONG-ARM MAN NAMED WA'AT ALAHF. THIS FELLOW, DESPITE HIS NAME, DIDN'T LAUGH VERY OFTEN.
ALWAYS FOR PHOTOS.
I WANT TO BE CALIPH INSTEAD OF THE CALIPH!
WHILE THE CALIPH OF BAGHDAD, THE GOOD HAROUN AL PLASSID, WHO HAD ABSOLUTE CONFIDENCE IN HIS GRAND VIZIER, PASSED HIS HAPPY, SLEEPY DAYS IN THE SWEET SERENITY OF HIS SOVEREIGNTY.
I AM AT PEACE.
TABARY

NOW THEN, TO BAGHDAD THE MAGNIFICENT...

THE ADVENTURES OF THE GRAND VIZIER IZNOGOUD
BY GOSCINNY & TABARY

IZNOGOUD
AND
THE DAY
OF MISRULE

SCRIPT: GOSCINNY   **DRAWING: TABARY**

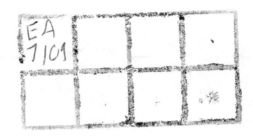
Original title: Le jour des fous

Original edition: © Dargaud Editeur Paris, 1972, by Goscinny & Tabary
www.dargaud.com

Lettering and text layout: Imadjinn sarl
Printed in Spain by Just Colour Graphic

This edition published in Great Britain in 2009 by
CINEBOOK Ltd
56 Beech Avenue
Canterbury, Kent
CT4 7TA
www.cinebook.com

A CIP catalogue record for this book
is available from the British Library

ISBN 978-1-905460-79-3

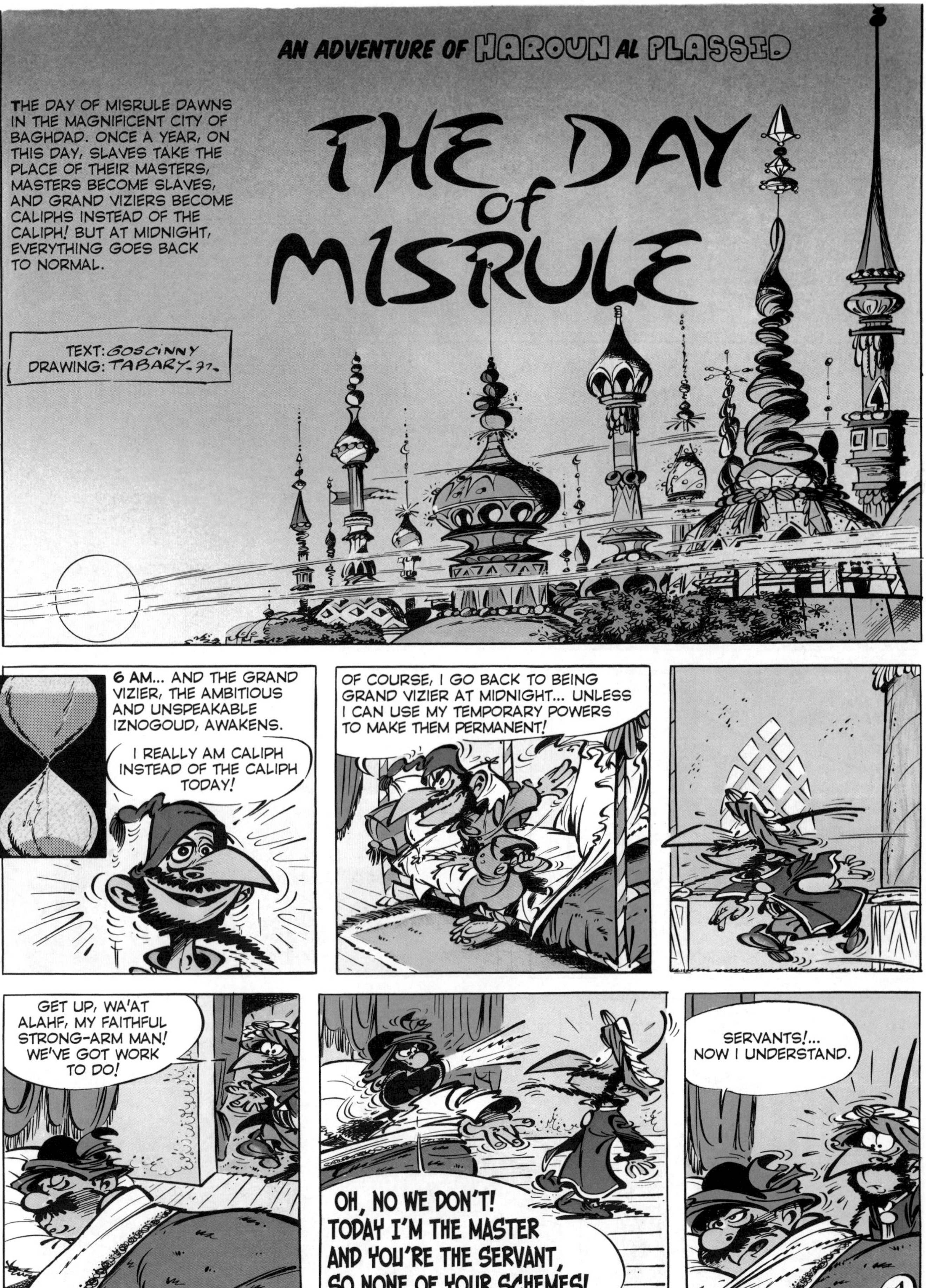
AN ADVENTURE OF HAROUN AL PLASSID
THE DAY of MISRULE
THE DAY OF MISRULE DAWNS IN THE MAGNIFICENT CITY OF BAGHDAD. ONCE A YEAR, ON THIS DAY, SLAVES TAKE THE PLACE OF THEIR MASTERS, MASTERS BECOME SLAVES, AND GRAND VIZIERS BECOME CALIPHS INSTEAD OF THE CALIPH! BUT AT MIDNIGHT, EVERYTHING GOES BACK TO NORMAL.
TEXT: GOSCINNY
DRAWING: TABARY-71.
6 AM... AND THE GRAND VIZIER, THE AMBITIOUS AND UNSPEAKABLE IZNOGOUD, AWAKENS.
I REALLY AM CALIPH INSTEAD OF THE CALIPH TODAY!
OF COURSE, I GO BACK TO BEING GRAND VIZIER AT MIDNIGHT... UNLESS I CAN USE MY TEMPORARY POWERS TO MAKE THEM PERMANENT!
GET UP, WA'AT ALAHF, MY FAITHFUL STRONG-ARM MAN! WE'VE GOT WORK TO DO!
OH, NO WE DON'T! TODAY I'M THE MASTER AND YOU'RE THE SERVANT, SO NONE OF YOUR SCHEMES!
SERVANTS!... NOW I UNDERSTAND.
1

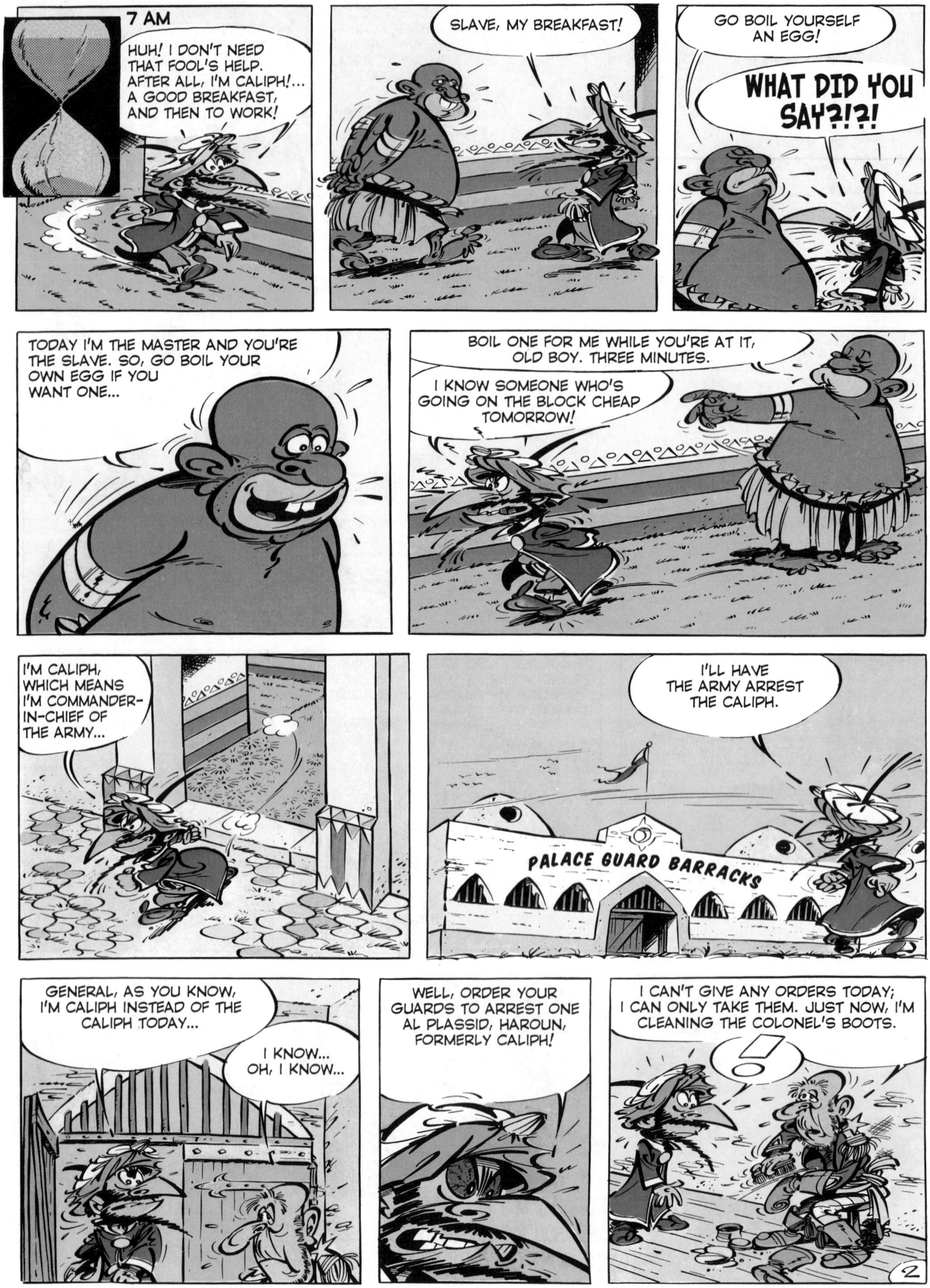
7 AM
HUH! I DON'T NEED THAT FOOL'S HELP. AFTER ALL, I'M CALIPH!... A GOOD BREAKFAST, AND THEN TO WORK!
SLAVE, MY BREAKFAST!
GO BOIL YOURSELF AN EGG!
WHAT DID YOU SAY?!?!
TODAY I'M THE MASTER AND YOU'RE THE SLAVE. SO, GO BOIL YOUR OWN EGG IF YOU WANT ONE...
BOIL ONE FOR ME WHILE YOU'RE AT IT, OLD BOY. THREE MINUTES.
I KNOW SOMEONE WHO'S GOING ON THE BLOCK CHEAP TOMORROW!
I'M CALIPH, WHICH MEANS I'M COMMANDER-IN-CHIEF OF THE ARMY...
I'LL HAVE THE ARMY ARREST THE CALIPH.
PALACE GUARD BARRACKS
GENERAL, AS YOU KNOW, I'M CALIPH INSTEAD OF THE CALIPH TODAY...
I KNOW... OH, I KNOW...
WELL, ORDER YOUR GUARDS TO ARREST ONE AL PLASSID, HAROUN, FORMERLY CALIPH!
I CAN'T GIVE ANY ORDERS TODAY; I CAN ONLY TAKE THEM. JUST NOW, I'M CLEANING THE COLONEL'S BOOTS.
!
2

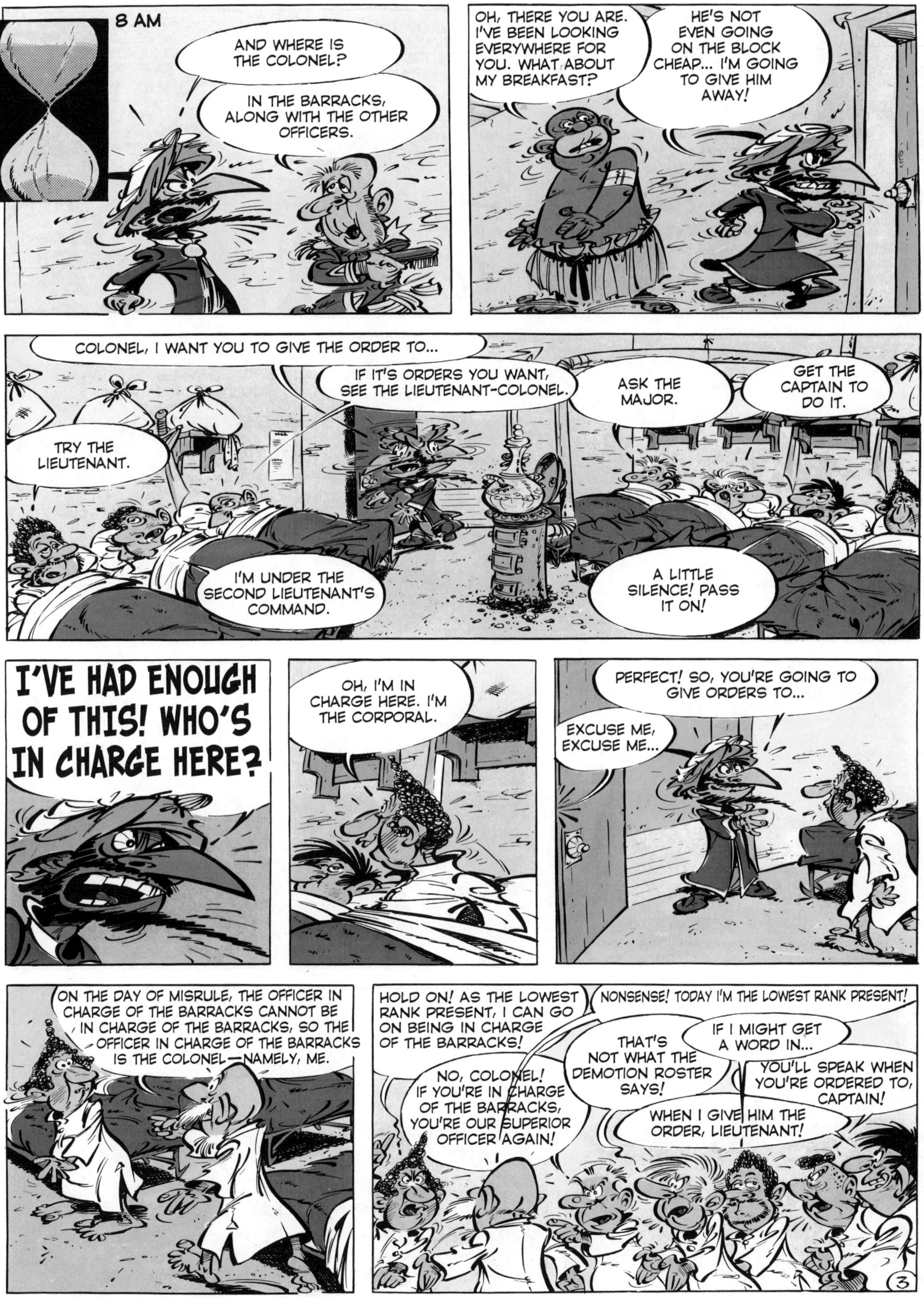
8 AM
AND WHERE IS THE COLONEL?
IN THE BARRACKS, ALONG WITH THE OTHER OFFICERS.
OH, THERE YOU ARE. I'VE BEEN LOOKING EVERYWHERE FOR YOU. WHAT ABOUT MY BREAKFAST?
HE'S NOT EVEN GOING ON THE BLOCK CHEAP... I'M GOING TO GIVE HIM AWAY!
COLONEL, I WANT YOU TO GIVE THE ORDER TO...
IF IT'S ORDERS YOU WANT, SEE THE LIEUTENANT-COLONEL.
ASK THE MAJOR.
GET THE CAPTAIN TO DO IT.
TRY THE LIEUTENANT.
I'M UNDER THE SECOND LIEUTENANT'S COMMAND.
A LITTLE SILENCE! PASS IT ON!
I'VE HAD ENOUGH OF THIS! WHO'S IN CHARGE HERE?
OH, I'M IN CHARGE HERE. I'M THE CORPORAL.
PERFECT! SO, YOU'RE GOING TO GIVE ORDERS TO...
EXCUSE ME, EXCUSE ME...
ON THE DAY OF MISRULE, THE OFFICER IN CHARGE OF THE BARRACKS CANNOT BE IN CHARGE OF THE BARRACKS, SO THE OFFICER IN CHARGE OF THE BARRACKS IS THE COLONEL—NAMELY, ME.
HOLD ON! AS THE LOWEST RANK PRESENT, I CAN GO ON BEING IN CHARGE OF THE BARRACKS!
NO, COLONEL! IF YOU'RE IN CHARGE OF THE BARRACKS, YOU'RE OUR SUPERIOR OFFICER AGAIN!
NONSENSE! TODAY I'M THE LOWEST RANK PRESENT!
THAT'S NOT WHAT THE DEMOTION ROSTER SAYS!
IF I MIGHT GET A WORD IN...
YOU'LL SPEAK WHEN YOU'RE ORDERED TO, CAPTAIN!
WHEN I GIVE HIM THE ORDER, LIEUTENANT!
3

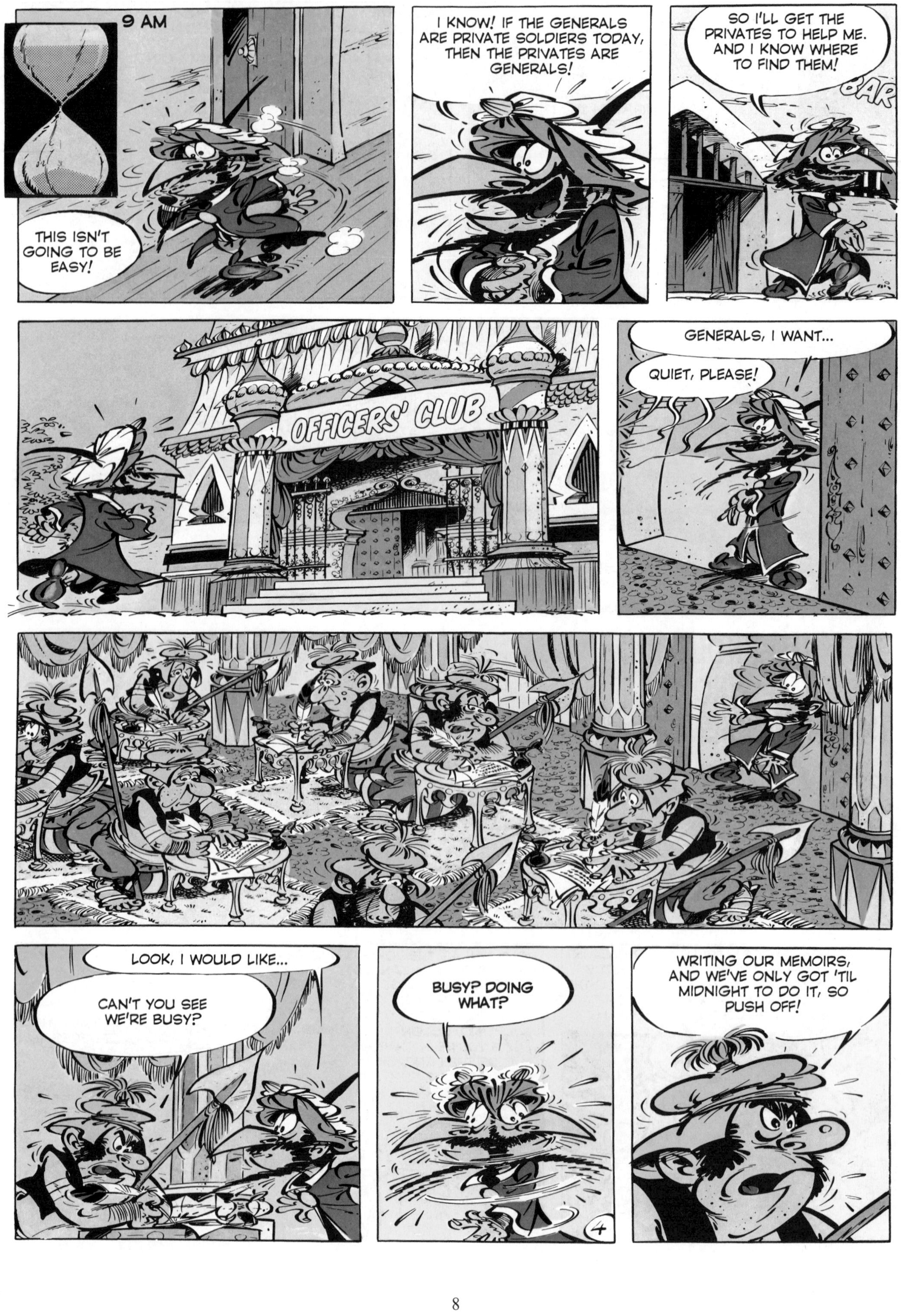
9 AM
THIS ISN'T GOING TO BE EASY!
I KNOW! IF THE GENERALS ARE PRIVATE SOLDIERS TODAY, THEN THE PRIVATES ARE GENERALS!
SO I'LL GET THE PRIVATES TO HELP ME. AND I KNOW WHERE TO FIND THEM!
BAR
OFFICERS' CLUB
GENERALS, I WANT...
QUIET, PLEASE!
LOOK, I WOULD LIKE...
CAN'T YOU SEE WE'RE BUSY?
BUSY? DOING WHAT?
WRITING OUR MEMOIRS, AND WE'VE ONLY GOT 'TIL MIDNIGHT TO DO IT, SO PUSH OFF!

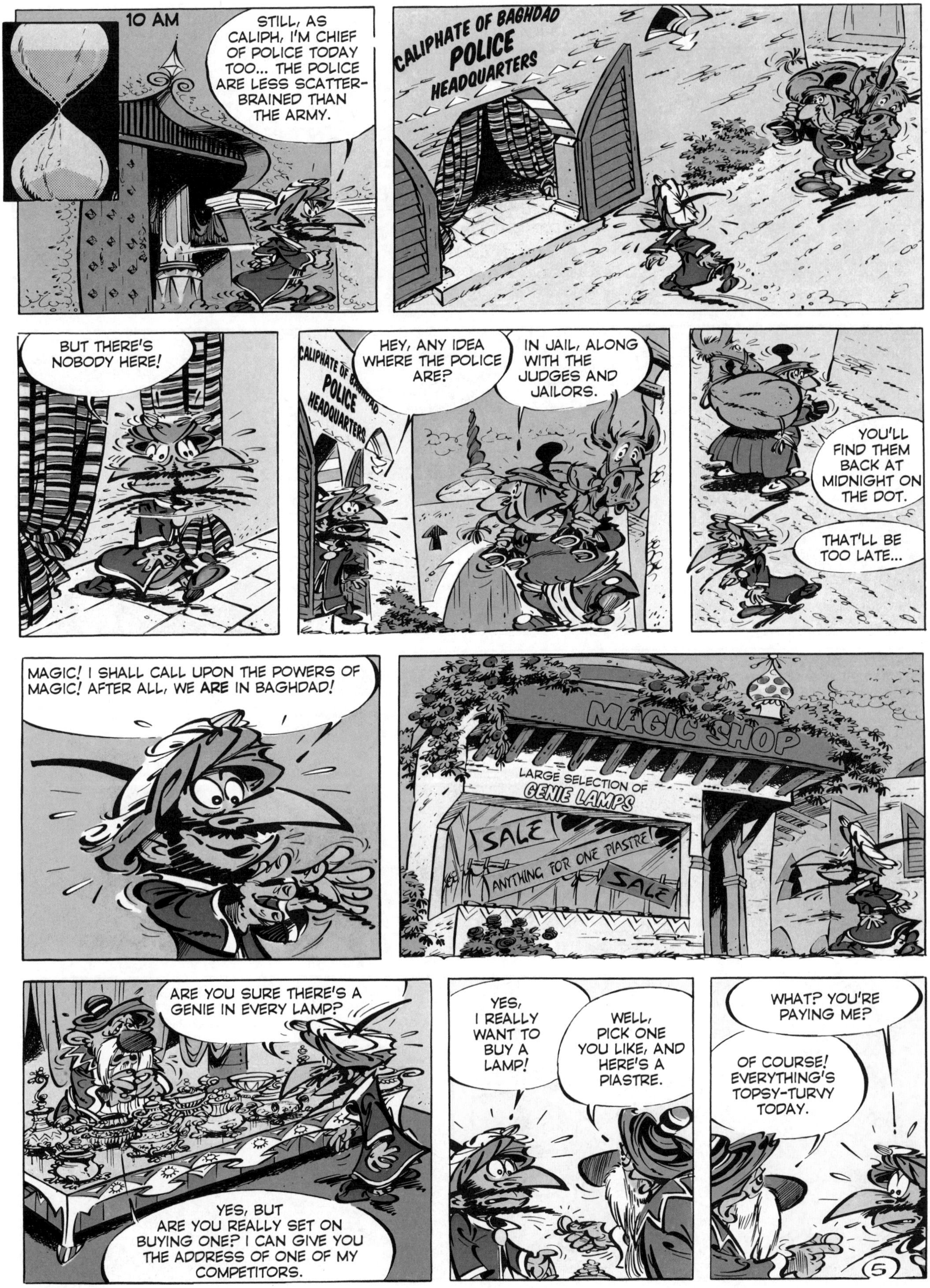
10 AM
STILL, AS CALIPH, I'M CHIEF OF POLICE TODAY TOO... THE POLICE ARE LESS SCATTER-BRAINED THAN THE ARMY.
CALIPHATE OF BAGHDAD POLICE HEADQUARTERS
BUT THERE'S NOBODY HERE!
CALIPHATE OF BAGHDAD POLICE HEADQUARTERS
HEY, ANY IDEA WHERE THE POLICE ARE?
IN JAIL, ALONG WITH THE JUDGES AND JAILORS.
YOU'LL FIND THEM BACK AT MIDNIGHT ON THE DOT.
THAT'LL BE TOO LATE...
MAGIC! I SHALL CALL UPON THE POWERS OF MAGIC! AFTER ALL, WE ARE IN BAGHDAD!
MAGIC SHOP
LARGE SELECTION OF GENIE LAMPS
SALE
ANYTHING FOR ONE PIASTRE
SALE
ARE YOU SURE THERE'S A GENIE IN EVERY LAMP?
YES, BUT ARE YOU REALLY SET ON BUYING ONE? I CAN GIVE YOU THE ADDRESS OF ONE OF MY COMPETITORS.
YES, I REALLY WANT TO BUY A LAMP!
WELL, PICK ONE YOU LIKE, AND HERE'S A PIASTRE.
WHAT? YOU'RE PAYING ME?
OF COURSE! EVERYTHING'S TOPSY-TURVY TODAY.
5

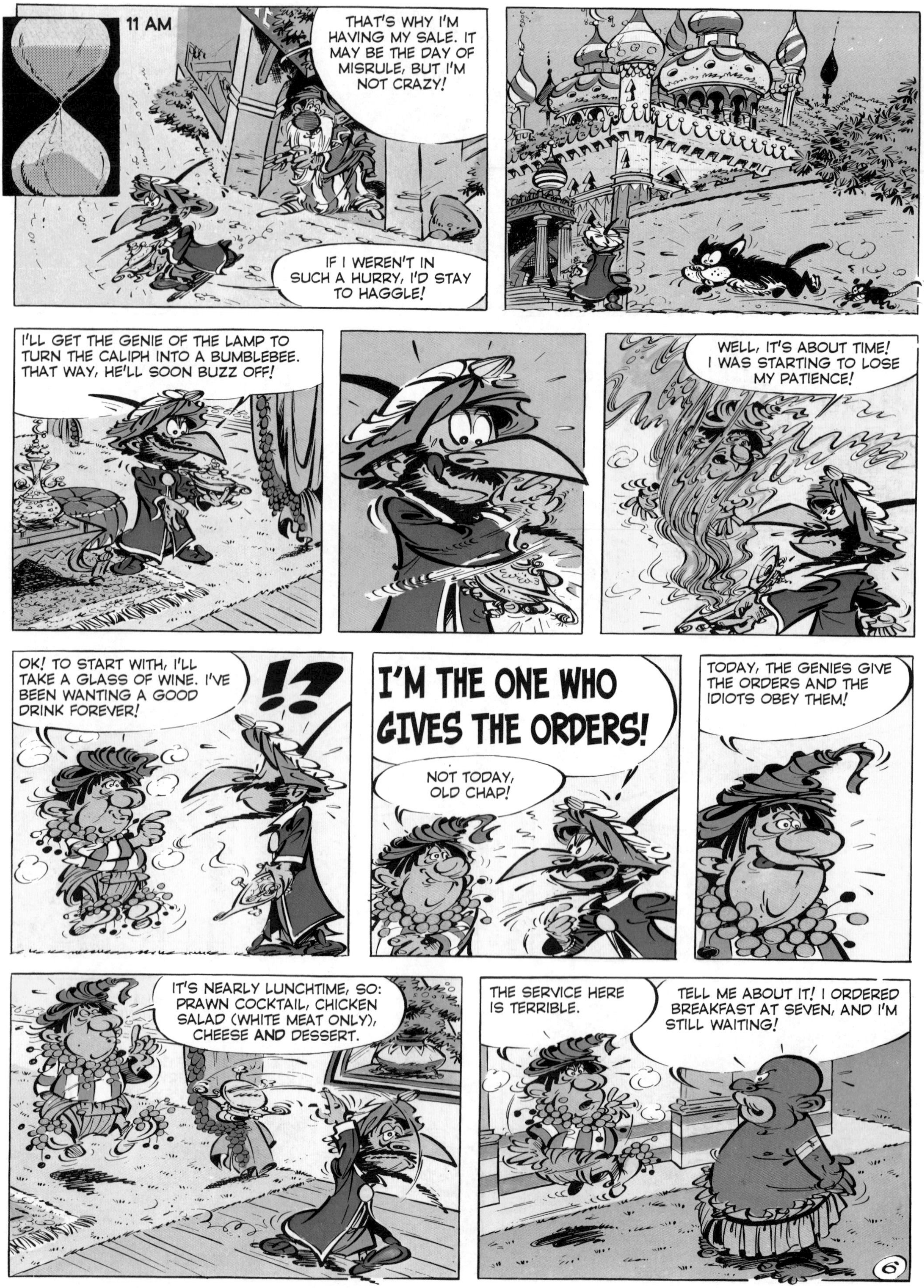
11 AM
THAT'S WHY I'M HAVING MY SALE. IT MAY BE THE DAY OF MISRULE, BUT I'M NOT CRAZY!
IF I WEREN'T IN SUCH A HURRY, I'D STAY TO HAGGLE!
I'LL GET THE GENIE OF THE LAMP TO TURN THE CALIPH INTO A BUMBLEBEE. THAT WAY, HE'LL SOON BUZZ OFF!
WELL, IT'S ABOUT TIME! I WAS STARTING TO LOSE MY PATIENCE!
OK! TO START WITH, I'LL TAKE A GLASS OF WINE. I'VE BEEN WANTING A GOOD DRINK FOREVER!
!?
I'M THE ONE WHO GIVES THE ORDERS!
NOT TODAY, OLD CHAP!
TODAY, THE GENIES GIVE THE ORDERS AND THE IDIOTS OBEY THEM!
IT'S NEARLY LUNCHTIME, SO: PRAWN COCKTAIL, CHICKEN SALAD (WHITE MEAT ONLY), CHEESE AND DESSERT.
THE SERVICE HERE IS TERRIBLE.
TELL ME ABOUT IT! I ORDERED BREAKFAST AT SEVEN, AND I'M STILL WAITING!
6

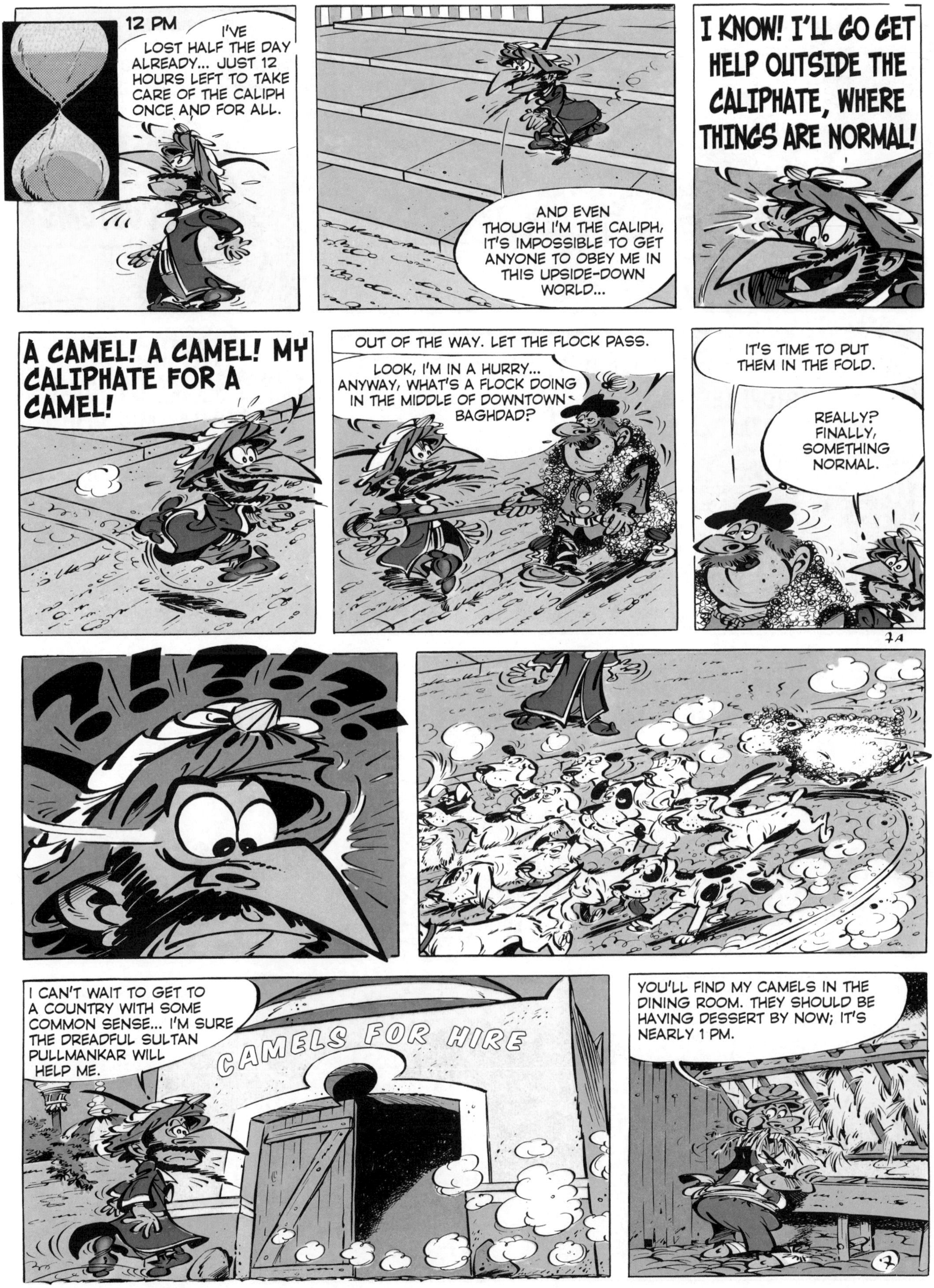
12 PM
I'VE LOST HALF THE DAY ALREADY... JUST 12 HOURS LEFT TO TAKE CARE OF THE CALIPH ONCE AND FOR ALL.
AND EVEN THOUGH I'M THE CALIPH, IT'S IMPOSSIBLE TO GET ANYONE TO OBEY ME IN THIS UPSIDE-DOWN WORLD...
I KNOW! I'LL GO GET HELP OUTSIDE THE CALIPHATE, WHERE THINGS ARE NORMAL!
A CAMEL! A CAMEL! MY CALIPHATE FOR A CAMEL!
OUT OF THE WAY. LET THE FLOCK PASS.
LOOK, I'M IN A HURRY... ANYWAY, WHAT'S A FLOCK DOING IN THE MIDDLE OF DOWNTOWN BAGHDAD?
IT'S TIME TO PUT THEM IN THE FOLD.
REALLY? FINALLY, SOMETHING NORMAL.
?!?!?!?!
I CAN'T WAIT TO GET TO A COUNTRY WITH SOME COMMON SENSE... I'M SURE THE DREADFUL SULTAN PULLMANKAR WILL HELP ME.
CAMELS FOR HIRE
YOU'LL FIND MY CAMELS IN THE DINING ROOM. THEY SHOULD BE HAVING DESSERT BY NOW; IT'S NEARLY 1 PM.

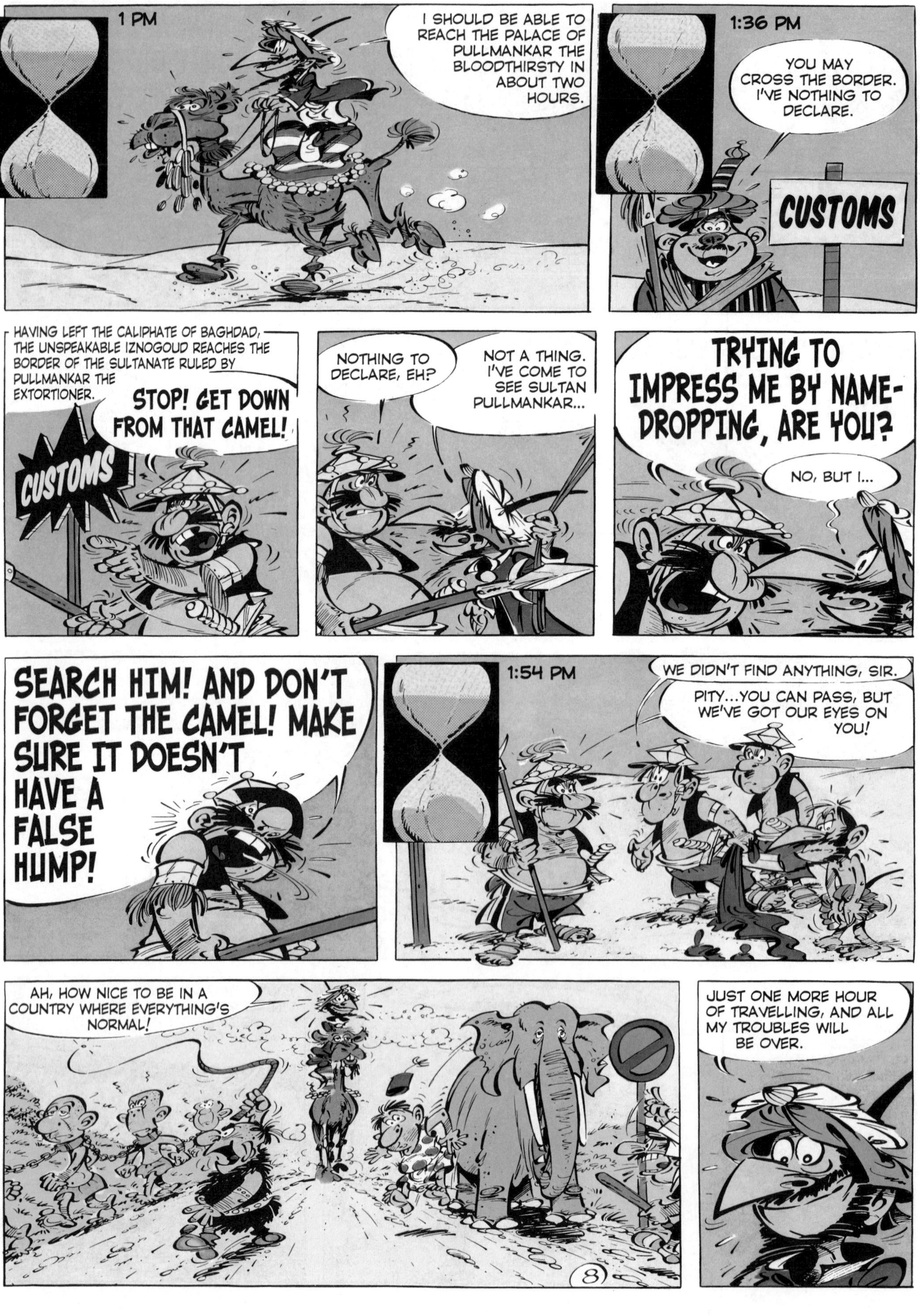
1 PM
I SHOULD BE ABLE TO REACH THE PALACE OF PULLMANKAR THE BLOODTHIRSTY IN ABOUT TWO HOURS.
1:36 PM
YOU MAY CROSS THE BORDER. I'VE NOTHING TO DECLARE.
CUSTOMS
HAVING LEFT THE CALIPHATE OF BAGHDAD, THE UNSPEAKABLE IZNOGOUD REACHES THE BORDER OF THE SULTANATE RULED BY PULLMANKAR THE EXTORTIONER.
STOP! GET DOWN FROM THAT CAMEL!
CUSTOMS
NOTHING TO DECLARE, EH?
NOT A THING. I'VE COME TO SEE SULTAN PULLMANKAR...
TRYING TO IMPRESS ME BY NAME-DROPPING, ARE YOU?
NO, BUT I...
SEARCH HIM! AND DON'T FORGET THE CAMEL! MAKE SURE IT DOESN'T HAVE A FALSE HUMP!
1:54 PM
WE DIDN'T FIND ANYTHING, SIR.
PITY...YOU CAN PASS, BUT WE'VE GOT OUR EYES ON YOU!
AH, HOW NICE TO BE IN A COUNTRY WHERE EVERYTHING'S NORMAL!
8
JUST ONE MORE HOUR OF TRAVELLING, AND ALL MY TROUBLES WILL BE OVER.

2 PM

ZZZ
ZZZZZ
ZZZZ

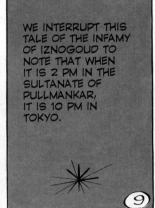

WE INTERRUPT THIS TALE OF THE INFAMY OF IZNOGOUD TO NOTE THAT WHEN IT IS 2 PM IN THE SULTANATE OF PULLMANKAR, IT IS 10 PM IN TOKYO.

⑨

3 PM

TO CONTINUE OUR STORY...

AH, HA! THE PALACE OF PULLMANKAR THE MONSTROUS!

TELL THE SULTAN THAT THE CALIPH OF BAGHDAD WISHES TO SEE HIM.

THE CALIPH OF BAGHDAD? AHKLOUB.*

*AN EXCLAMATION OF SURPRISE, COMMON IN THE SULTANATE

THE CALIPH OF BAGHDAD, COMMANDER OF THE FAITHFUL!

AH, MY DEAR COLLEAGUE!

WHAT'S ALL THIS? YOU'RE NOT THE CALIPH—YOU'RE ONLY THE REVOLTING GRAND VIZIER IZNOGOUD!

3:27 PM

I DON'T LIKE PRACTICAL JOKES. HAVE HIM IMPALED, BOYS!

JUST GIVE ME FIVE MINUTES... I CAN EXPLAIN EVERYTHING!

3:32 PM

FINE. SO YOU'RE CALIPH UNTIL MIDNIGHT. AND THEN WHAT?

AND THEN IT'S UP TO YOU WHETHER I REMAIN CALIPH FOR GOOD.

I'LL OPEN THE BORDERS OF THE CALIPHATE TO YOU, YOUR ARMY WILL SEIZE THE CALIPH, AND I SHALL BECOME IZNOGOUD THE GREAT, CALIPH OF BAGHDAD!

AND WHAT'S IN IT FOR ME? AFTER ALL, HAROUN AL PLASSID IS MY DEAR FRIEND—MY BELOVED COUSIN.

I THOUGHT YOU'D ASK THAT...

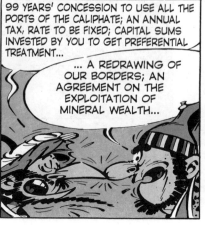

99 YEARS' CONCESSION TO USE ALL THE PORTS OF THE CALIPHATE; AN ANNUAL TAX, RATE TO BE FIXED; CAPITAL SUMS INVESTED BY YOU TO GET PREFERENTIAL TREATMENT...

... A REDRAWING OF OUR BORDERS; AN AGREEMENT ON THE EXPLOITATION OF MINERAL WEALTH...

... AND CULTURAL EXCHANGES!

AND CULTURAL EXCHANGES! DONE, MY DEAR GREAT!

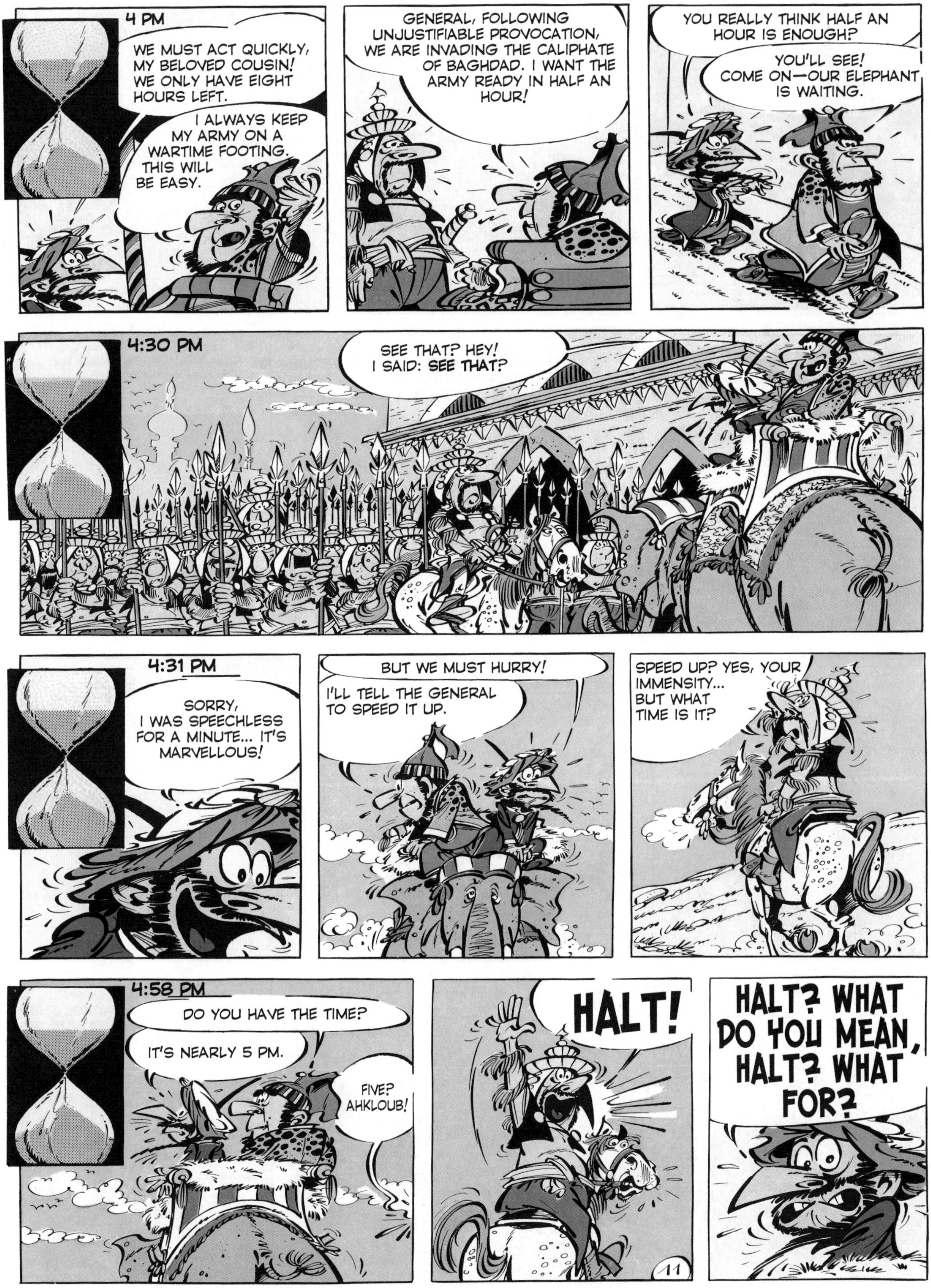
4 PM
WE MUST ACT QUICKLY, MY BELOVED COUSIN! WE ONLY HAVE EIGHT HOURS LEFT.
I ALWAYS KEEP MY ARMY ON A WARTIME FOOTING. THIS WILL BE EASY.
GENERAL, FOLLOWING UNJUSTIFIABLE PROVOCATION, WE ARE INVADING THE CALIPHATE OF BAGHDAD. I WANT THE ARMY READY IN HALF AN HOUR!
YOU REALLY THINK HALF AN HOUR IS ENOUGH?
YOU'LL SEE! COME ON—OUR ELEPHANT IS WAITING.
4:30 PM
SEE THAT? HEY! I SAID: SEE THAT?
4:31 PM
SORRY, I WAS SPEECHLESS FOR A MINUTE... IT'S MARVELLOUS!
BUT WE MUST HURRY!
I'LL TELL THE GENERAL TO SPEED IT UP.
SPEED UP? YES, YOUR IMMENSITY... BUT WHAT TIME IS IT?
4:58 PM
DO YOU HAVE THE TIME?
IT'S NEARLY 5 PM.
FIVE? AHKLOUB!
HALT!
HALT? WHAT DO YOU MEAN, HALT? WHAT FOR?
11

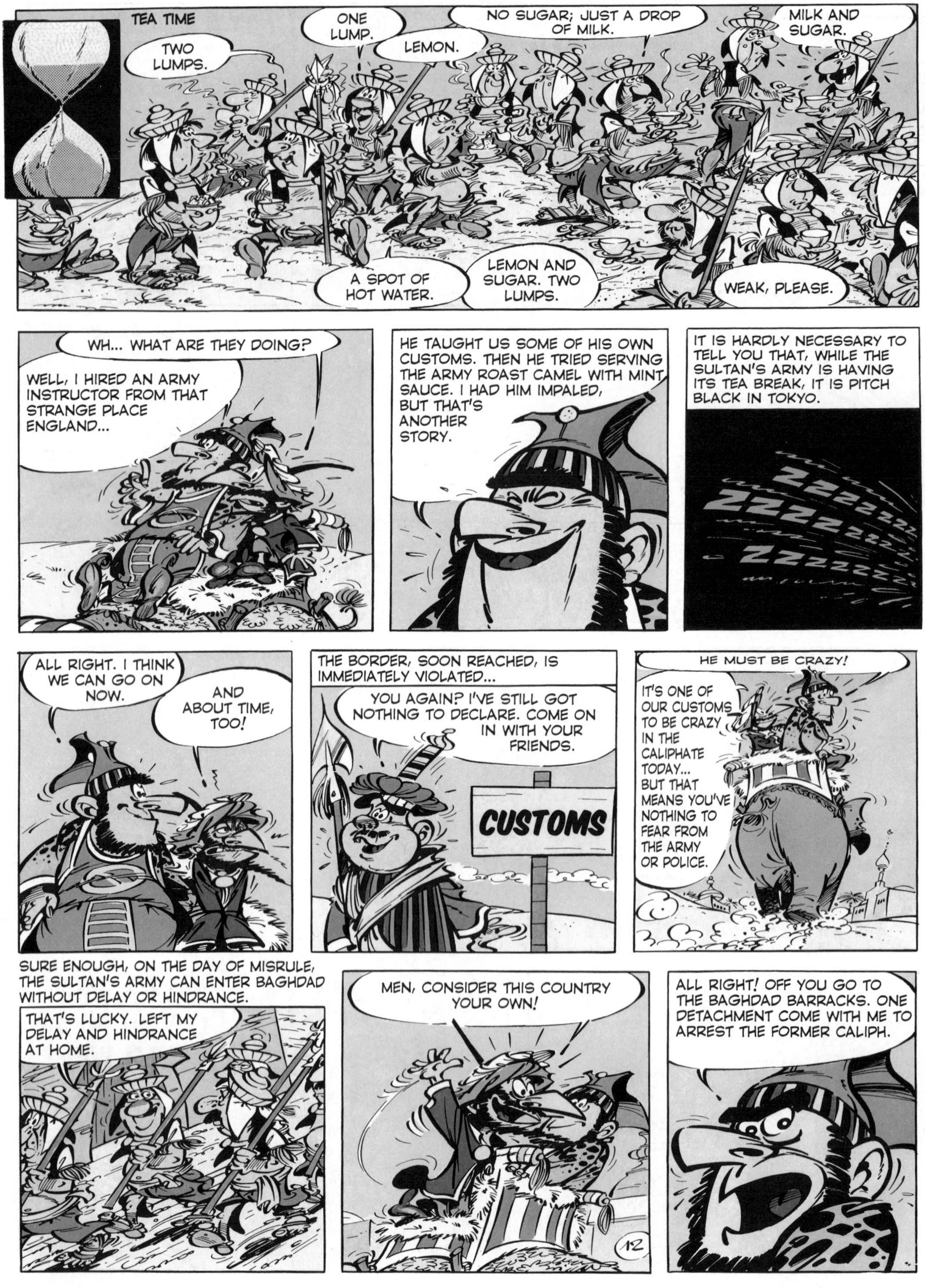
TEA TIME
TWO LUMPS.
ONE LUMP.
LEMON.
NO SUGAR; JUST A DROP OF MILK.
MILK AND SUGAR.
A SPOT OF HOT WATER.
LEMON AND SUGAR. TWO LUMPS.
WEAK, PLEASE.
WH... WHAT ARE THEY DOING?
WELL, I HIRED AN ARMY INSTRUCTOR FROM THAT STRANGE PLACE ENGLAND...
HE TAUGHT US SOME OF HIS OWN CUSTOMS. THEN HE TRIED SERVING THE ARMY ROAST CAMEL WITH MINT SAUCE. I HAD HIM IMPALED, BUT THAT'S ANOTHER STORY.
IT IS HARDLY NECESSARY TO TELL YOU THAT, WHILE THE SULTAN'S ARMY IS HAVING ITS TEA BREAK, IT IS PITCH BLACK IN TOKYO.
ZZZZZZZ
ALL RIGHT. I THINK WE CAN GO ON NOW.
AND ABOUT TIME, TOO!
THE BORDER, SOON REACHED, IS IMMEDIATELY VIOLATED...
YOU AGAIN? I'VE STILL GOT NOTHING TO DECLARE. COME ON IN WITH YOUR FRIENDS.
CUSTOMS
HE MUST BE CRAZY!
IT'S ONE OF OUR CUSTOMS TO BE CRAZY IN THE CALIPHATE TODAY... BUT THAT MEANS YOU'VE NOTHING TO FEAR FROM THE ARMY OR POLICE.
SURE ENOUGH, ON THE DAY OF MISRULE, THE SULTAN'S ARMY CAN ENTER BAGHDAD WITHOUT DELAY OR HINDRANCE.
THAT'S LUCKY. LEFT MY DELAY AND HINDRANCE AT HOME.
MEN, CONSIDER THIS COUNTRY YOUR OWN!
ALL RIGHT! OFF YOU GO TO THE BAGHDAD BARRACKS. ONE DETACHMENT COME WITH ME TO ARREST THE FORMER CALIPH.
12

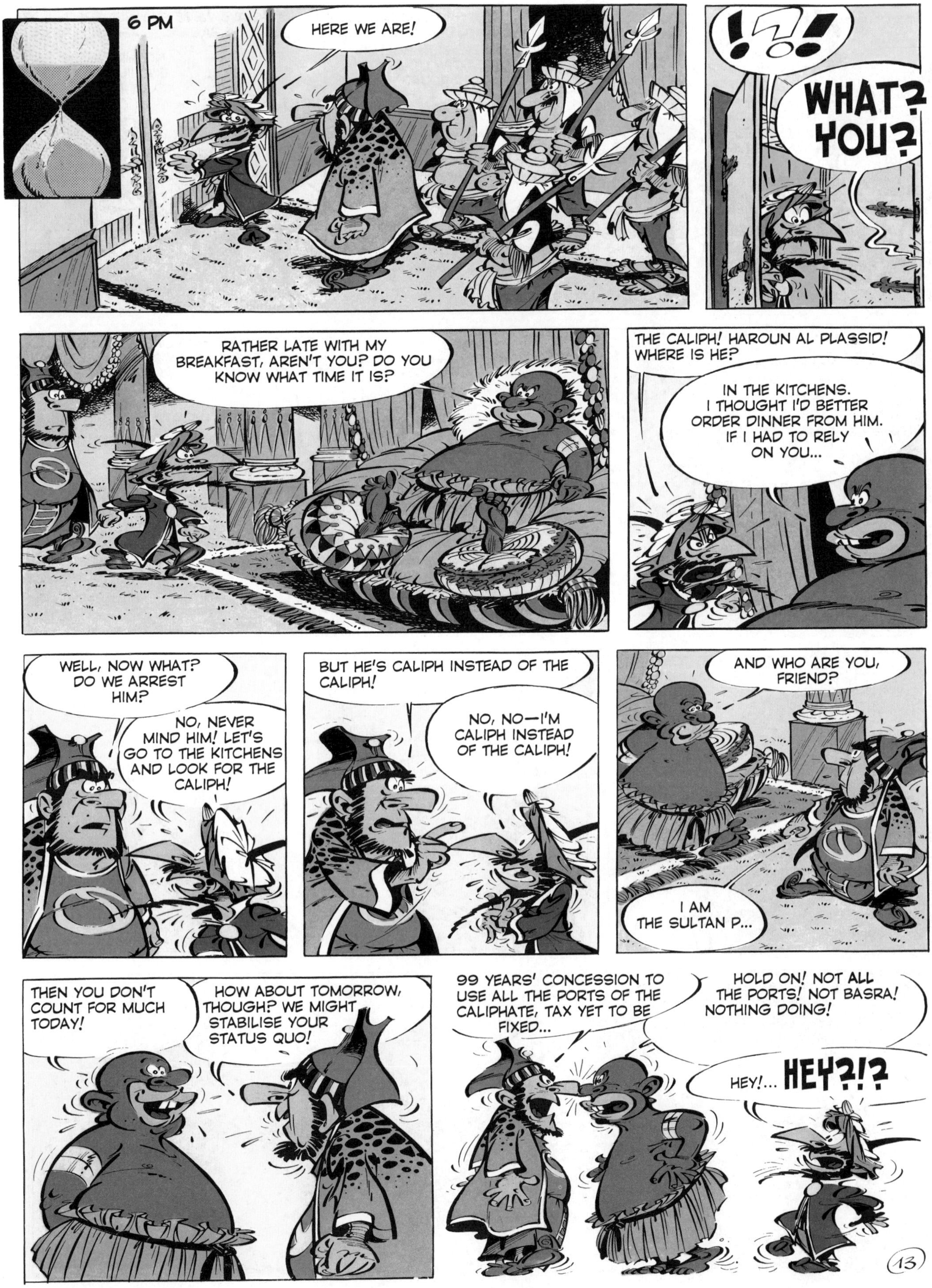
6 PM
HERE WE ARE!
!?!
WHAT? YOU?
RATHER LATE WITH MY BREAKFAST, AREN'T YOU? DO YOU KNOW WHAT TIME IT IS?
THE CALIPH! HAROUN AL PLASSID! WHERE IS HE?
IN THE KITCHENS. I THOUGHT I'D BETTER ORDER DINNER FROM HIM. IF I HAD TO RELY ON YOU...
WELL, NOW WHAT? DO WE ARREST HIM?
NO, NEVER MIND HIM! LET'S GO TO THE KITCHENS AND LOOK FOR THE CALIPH!
BUT HE'S CALIPH INSTEAD OF THE CALIPH!
NO, NO—I'M CALIPH INSTEAD OF THE CALIPH!
AND WHO ARE YOU, FRIEND?
I AM THE SULTAN P...
THEN YOU DON'T COUNT FOR MUCH TODAY!
HOW ABOUT TOMORROW, THOUGH? WE MIGHT STABILISE YOUR STATUS QUO!
99 YEARS' CONCESSION TO USE ALL THE PORTS OF THE CALIPHATE, TAX YET TO BE FIXED...
HOLD ON! NOT **ALL** THE PORTS! NOT BASRA! NOTHING DOING!
HEY!... HEY?!?
13

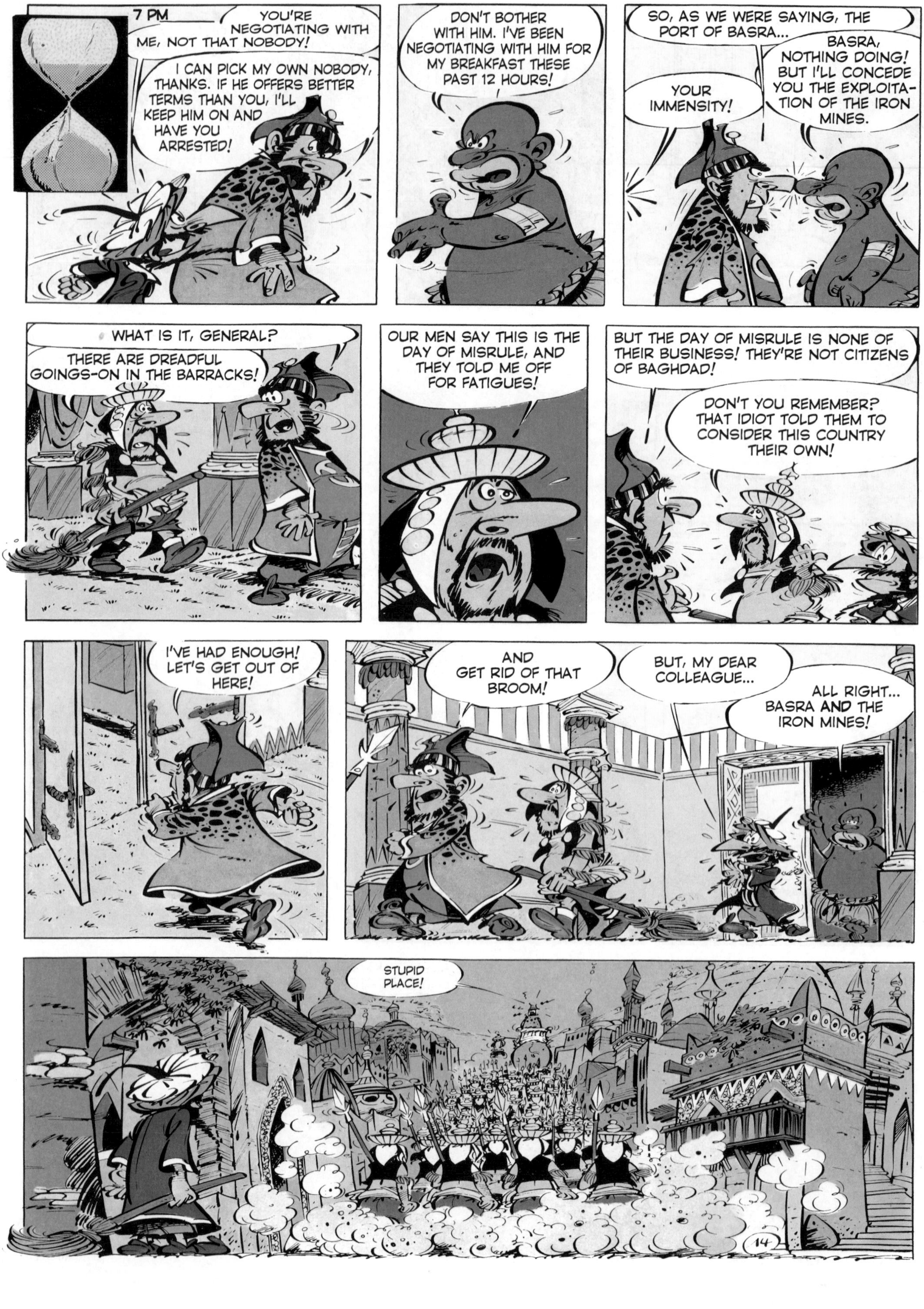
7 PM
YOU'RE NEGOTIATING WITH ME, NOT THAT NOBODY!
I CAN PICK MY OWN NOBODY, THANKS. IF HE OFFERS BETTER TERMS THAN YOU, I'LL KEEP HIM ON AND HAVE YOU ARRESTED!
DON'T BOTHER WITH HIM. I'VE BEEN NEGOTIATING WITH HIM FOR MY BREAKFAST THESE PAST 12 HOURS!
SO, AS WE WERE SAYING, THE PORT OF BASRA...
YOUR IMMENSITY!
BASRA, NOTHING DOING! BUT I'LL CONCEDE YOU THE EXPLOITATION OF THE IRON MINES.
WHAT IS IT, GENERAL?
THERE ARE DREADFUL GOINGS-ON IN THE BARRACKS!
OUR MEN SAY THIS IS THE DAY OF MISRULE, AND THEY TOLD ME OFF FOR FATIGUES!
BUT THE DAY OF MISRULE IS NONE OF THEIR BUSINESS! THEY'RE NOT CITIZENS OF BAGHDAD!
DON'T YOU REMEMBER? THAT IDIOT TOLD THEM TO CONSIDER THIS COUNTRY THEIR OWN!
I'VE HAD ENOUGH! LET'S GET OUT OF HERE!
AND GET RID OF THAT BROOM!
BUT, MY DEAR COLLEAGUE...
ALL RIGHT... BASRA AND THE IRON MINES!
STUPID PLACE!
14

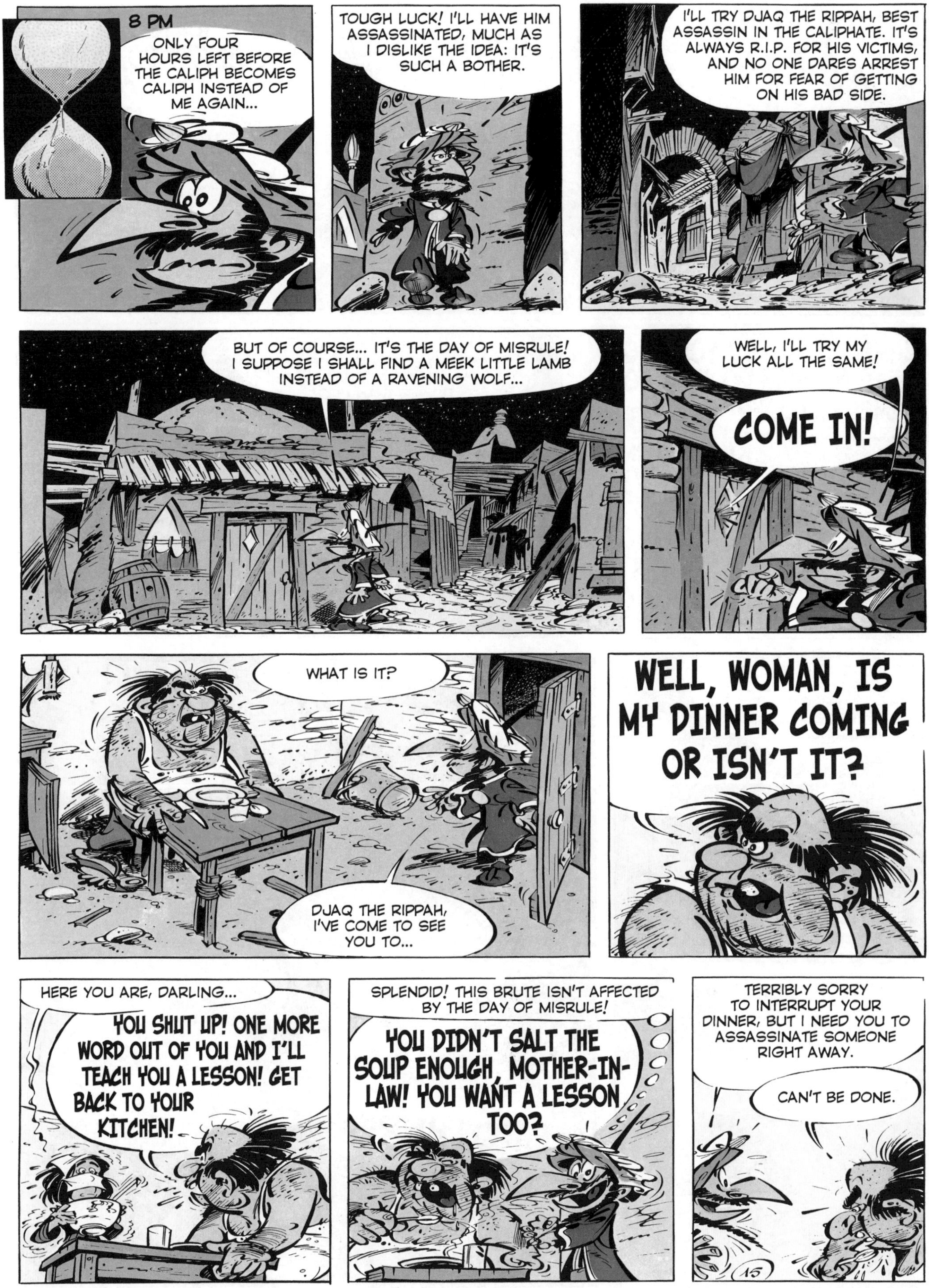

8 PM
ONLY FOUR HOURS LEFT BEFORE THE CALIPH BECOMES CALIPH INSTEAD OF ME AGAIN...
TOUGH LUCK! I'LL HAVE HIM ASSASSINATED, MUCH AS I DISLIKE THE IDEA: IT'S SUCH A BOTHER.
I'LL TRY DJAQ THE RIPPAH, BEST ASSASSIN IN THE CALIPHATE. IT'S ALWAYS R.I.P. FOR HIS VICTIMS, AND NO ONE DARES ARREST HIM FOR FEAR OF GETTING ON HIS BAD SIDE.
BUT OF COURSE... IT'S THE DAY OF MISRULE! I SUPPOSE I SHALL FIND A MEEK LITTLE LAMB INSTEAD OF A RAVENING WOLF...
WELL, I'LL TRY MY LUCK ALL THE SAME!
COME IN!
WHAT IS IT?
DJAQ THE RIPPAH, I'VE COME TO SEE YOU TO...
WELL, WOMAN, IS MY DINNER COMING OR ISN'T IT?
HERE YOU ARE, DARLING...
YOU SHUT UP! ONE MORE WORD OUT OF YOU AND I'LL TEACH YOU A LESSON! GET BACK TO YOUR KITCHEN!
SPLENDID! THIS BRUTE ISN'T AFFECTED BY THE DAY OF MISRULE!
YOU DIDN'T SALT THE SOUP ENOUGH, MOTHER-IN-LAW! YOU WANT A LESSON TOO?
TERRIBLY SORRY TO INTERRUPT YOUR DINNER, BUT I NEED YOU TO ASSASSINATE SOMEONE RIGHT AWAY.
CAN'T BE DONE.

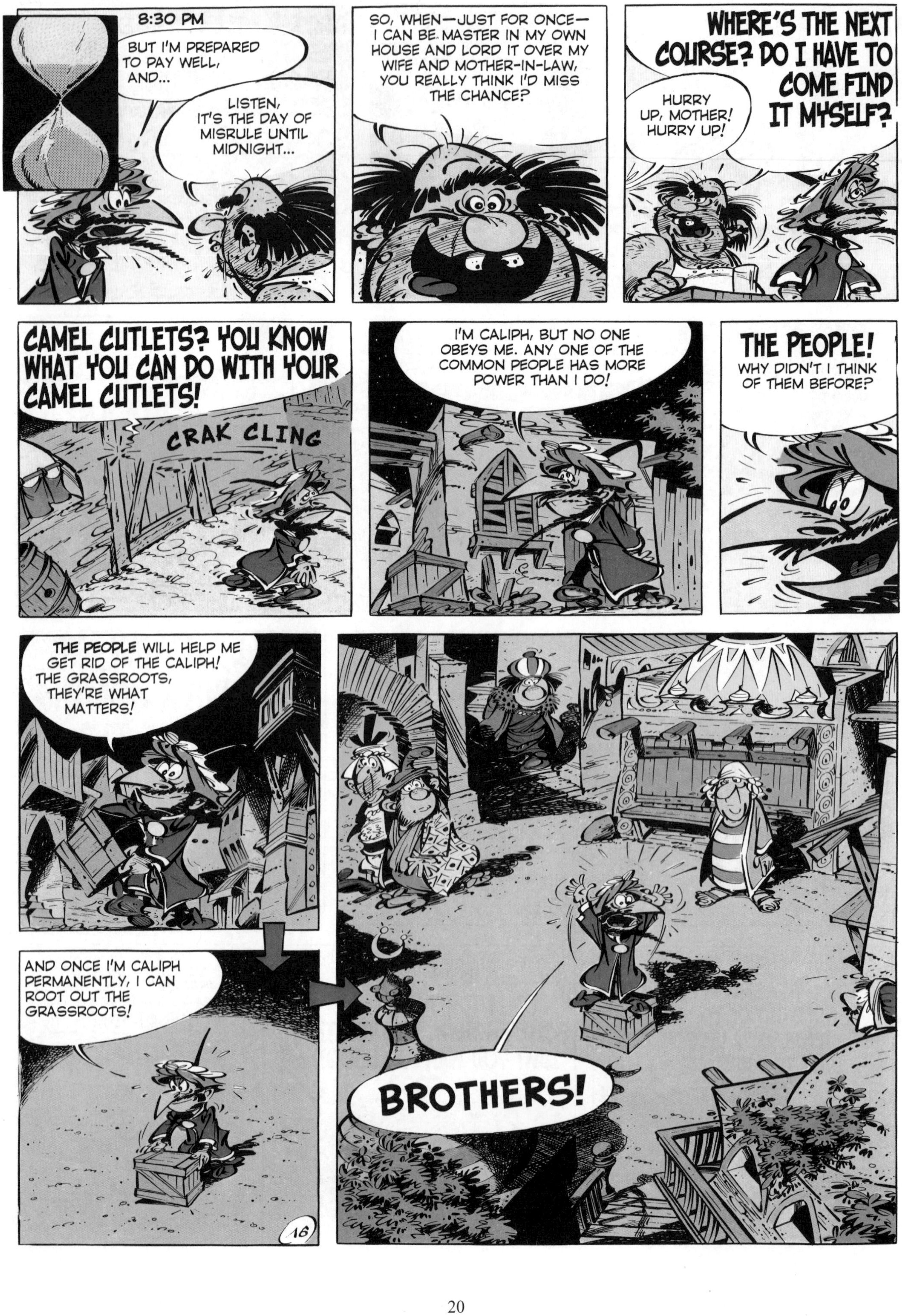
8:30 PM
BUT I'M PREPARED TO PAY WELL, AND...
LISTEN, IT'S THE DAY OF MISRULE UNTIL MIDNIGHT...
SO, WHEN—JUST FOR ONCE—I CAN BE MASTER IN MY OWN HOUSE AND LORD IT OVER MY WIFE AND MOTHER-IN-LAW, YOU REALLY THINK I'D MISS THE CHANCE?
WHERE'S THE NEXT COURSE? DO I HAVE TO COME FIND IT MYSELF?
HURRY UP, MOTHER! HURRY UP!
CAMEL CUTLETS? YOU KNOW WHAT YOU CAN DO WITH YOUR CAMEL CUTLETS!
CRAK CLING
I'M CALIPH, BUT NO ONE OBEYS ME. ANY ONE OF THE COMMON PEOPLE HAS MORE POWER THAN I DO!
THE PEOPLE! WHY DIDN'T I THINK OF THEM BEFORE?
THE PEOPLE WILL HELP ME GET RID OF THE CALIPH! THE GRASSROOTS, THEY'RE WHAT MATTERS!
AND ONCE I'M CALIPH PERMANENTLY, I CAN ROOT OUT THE GRASSROOTS!
16
BROTHERS!

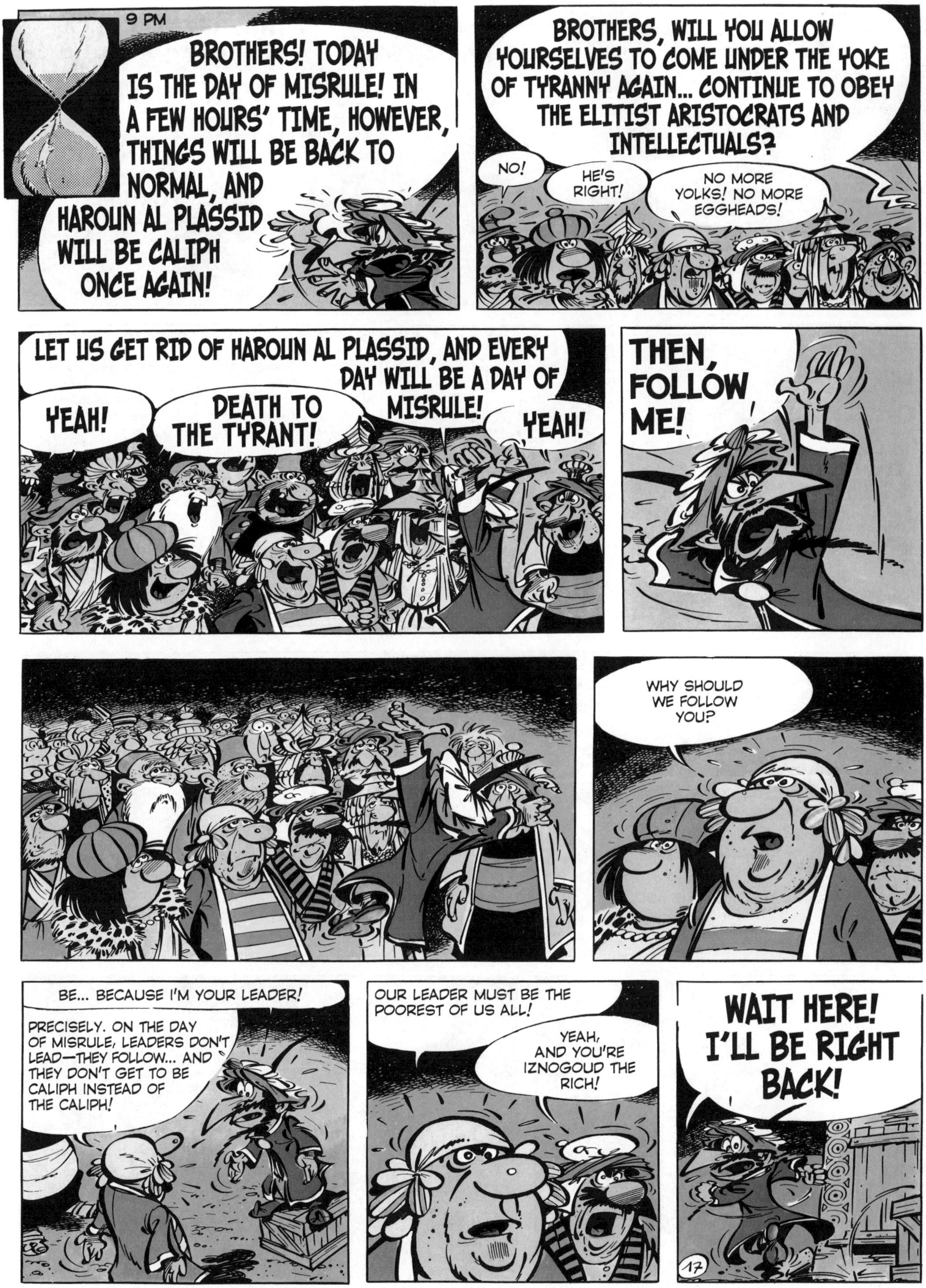
9 PM
BROTHERS! TODAY IS THE DAY OF MISRULE! IN A FEW HOURS' TIME, HOWEVER, THINGS WILL BE BACK TO NORMAL, AND HAROUN AL PLASSID WILL BE CALIPH ONCE AGAIN!
BROTHERS, WILL YOU ALLOW YOURSELVES TO COME UNDER THE YOKE OF TYRANNY AGAIN... CONTINUE TO OBEY THE ELITIST ARISTOCRATS AND INTELLECTUALS?
NO!
HE'S RIGHT!
NO MORE YOLKS! NO MORE EGGHEADS!
LET US GET RID OF HAROUN AL PLASSID, AND EVERY DAY WILL BE A DAY OF MISRULE!
YEAH!
DEATH TO THE TYRANT!
YEAH!
THEN, FOLLOW ME!
WHY SHOULD WE FOLLOW YOU?
BE... BECAUSE I'M YOUR LEADER!
PRECISELY. ON THE DAY OF MISRULE, LEADERS DON'T LEAD—THEY FOLLOW... AND THEY DON'T GET TO BE CALIPH INSTEAD OF THE CALIPH!
OUR LEADER MUST BE THE POOREST OF US ALL!
YEAH, AND YOU'RE IZNOGOUD THE RICH!
WAIT HERE! I'LL BE RIGHT BACK!
17

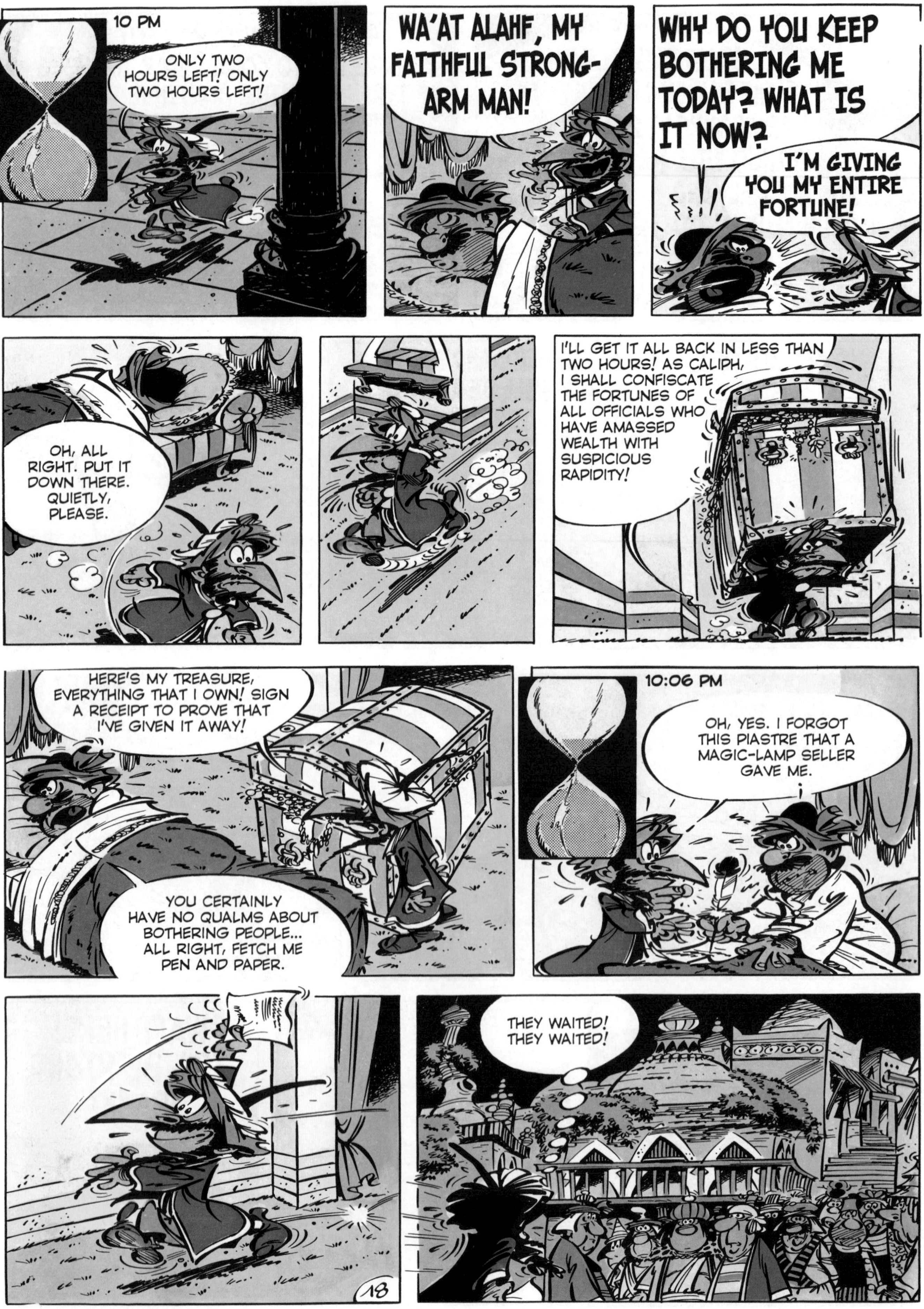

10 PM
ONLY TWO HOURS LEFT! ONLY TWO HOURS LEFT!
WA'AT ALAHF, MY FAITHFUL STRONG-ARM MAN!
WHY DO YOU KEEP BOTHERING ME TODAY? WHAT IS IT NOW?
I'M GIVING YOU MY ENTIRE FORTUNE!
OH, ALL RIGHT. PUT IT DOWN THERE. QUIETLY, PLEASE.
I'LL GET IT ALL BACK IN LESS THAN TWO HOURS! AS CALIPH, I SHALL CONFISCATE THE FORTUNES OF ALL OFFICIALS WHO HAVE AMASSED WEALTH WITH SUSPICIOUS RAPIDITY!
HERE'S MY TREASURE, EVERYTHING THAT I OWN! SIGN A RECEIPT TO PROVE THAT I'VE GIVEN IT AWAY!
YOU CERTAINLY HAVE NO QUALMS ABOUT BOTHERING PEOPLE... ALL RIGHT, FETCH ME PEN AND PAPER.
10:06 PM
OH, YES. I FORGOT THIS PIASTRE THAT A MAGIC-LAMP SELLER GAVE ME.
18
THEY WAITED! THEY WAITED!

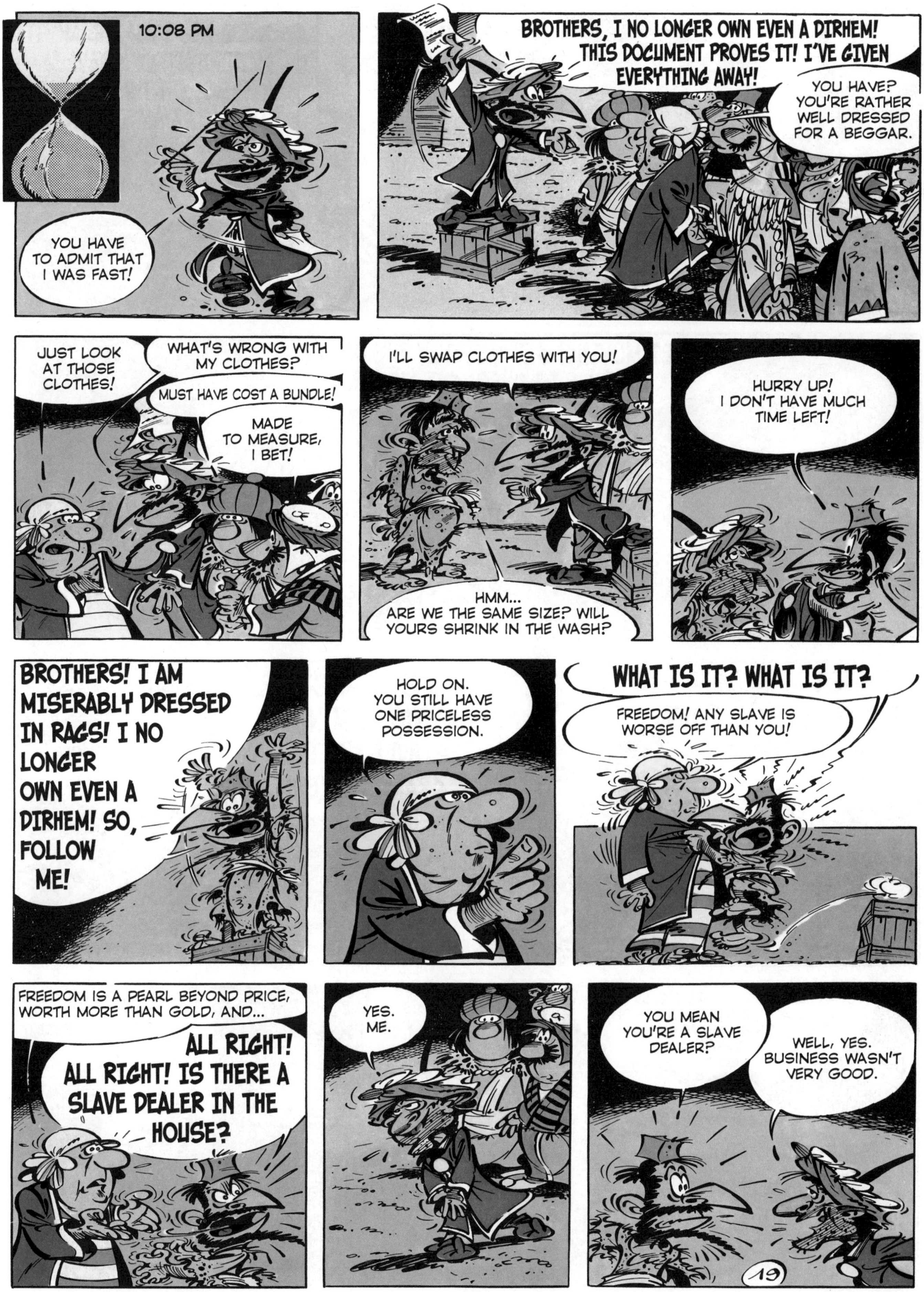
10:08 PM
YOU HAVE TO ADMIT THAT I WAS FAST!
BROTHERS, I NO LONGER OWN EVEN A DIRHEM! THIS DOCUMENT PROVES IT! I'VE GIVEN EVERYTHING AWAY!
YOU HAVE? YOU'RE RATHER WELL DRESSED FOR A BEGGAR.
JUST LOOK AT THOSE CLOTHES!
WHAT'S WRONG WITH MY CLOTHES?
MUST HAVE COST A BUNDLE!
MADE TO MEASURE, I BET!
I'LL SWAP CLOTHES WITH YOU!
HMM... ARE WE THE SAME SIZE? WILL YOURS SHRINK IN THE WASH?
HURRY UP! I DON'T HAVE MUCH TIME LEFT!
BROTHERS! I AM MISERABLY DRESSED IN RAGS! I NO LONGER OWN EVEN A DIRHEM! SO, FOLLOW ME!
HOLD ON. YOU STILL HAVE ONE PRICELESS POSSESSION.
WHAT IS IT? WHAT IS IT?
FREEDOM! ANY SLAVE IS WORSE OFF THAN YOU!
FREEDOM IS A PEARL BEYOND PRICE, WORTH MORE THAN GOLD, AND...
ALL RIGHT! ALL RIGHT! IS THERE A SLAVE DEALER IN THE HOUSE?
YES. ME.
YOU MEAN YOU'RE A SLAVE DEALER?
WELL, YES. BUSINESS WASN'T VERY GOOD.
19

11 PM

THEN, SELL ME AS A SLAVE! PLEASE!

HMM... YOU WON'T IMPROVE MY BOTTOM LINE MUCH...

STILL, I SEE YOU'RE ALREADY A SLAVE TO YOUR OBSESSION. I'LL DO YOU A GOOD TURN, BUT DON'T GET HOT UNDER THE COLLAR LATER...

CLICK

COMRADES, I AM THE MOST MISERABLE OF SLAVES! AND SO, ON THE DAY OF MISRULE, I AM THE MOST POWERFUL OF...

GET MOVING! GET MOVING! THE DAY OF MISRULE IS OVER! GET MOVING!

O... OVER, GENERAL? IT'S ONLY 11:00 PLUS A FEW GRAINS OF SAND!

WRONG, SLAVE. IT'S ONE SECOND PAST MIDNIGHT.

IT'S ALL A MISTAKE! ANYWAY, I'M NOT A SLAVE! I'M THE GRAND VIZIER!

THAT MAY HAVE BEEN SO WHILE IT WAS PM, BUT NOW THAT IT'S AM, LIFE IS BACK TO NORMAL. SO, DO AS YOUR MASTER SAYS, O MISERABLE SLAVE.

COME ON. I'M GOING TO SELL YOU AS A SLAVE ABROAD. YOU MIGHT FETCH MORE ON THE EXPORT MARKET.

ER... AS YOU WILL HAVE GATHERED, THIS TIMEPIECE WAS AN HOUR SLOW. WE SHOULD FURTHER EXPLAIN THAT OUR ARTIST SET IT BY HIS OWN WATCH... AND TAHBARI THE GREAT'S WATCH IS ALWAYS SLOW...

OH, LEALLY! SO THAT'S WHY I ALLIVED LATE AT THE OFFICE TODAY!

THE END GOSCINNY-TABARY-74

24

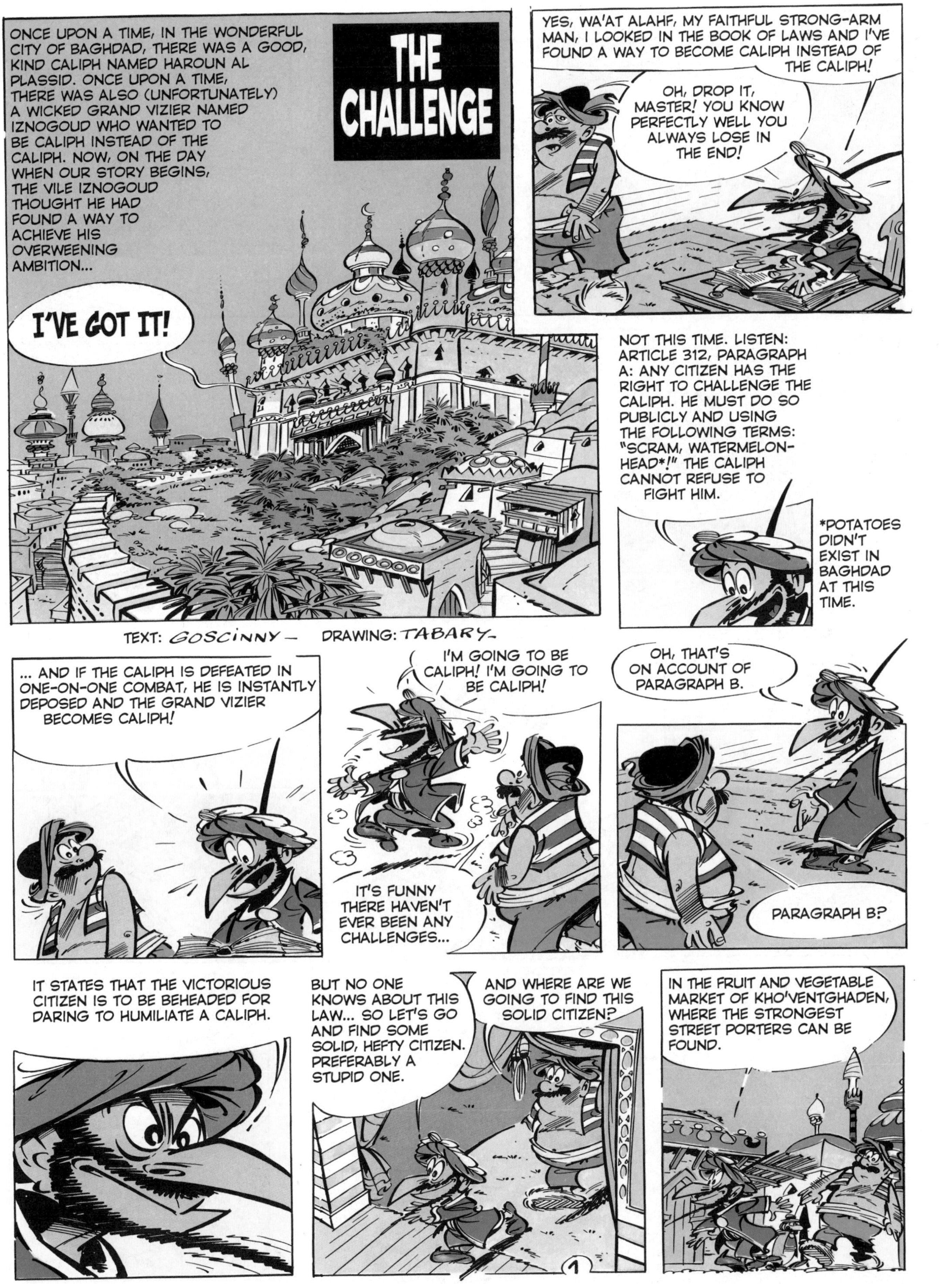
ONCE UPON A TIME, IN THE WONDERFUL CITY OF BAGHDAD, THERE WAS A GOOD, KIND CALIPH NAMED HAROUN AL PLASSID. ONCE UPON A TIME, THERE WAS ALSO (UNFORTUNATELY) A WICKED GRAND VIZIER NAMED IZNOGOUD WHO WANTED TO BE CALIPH INSTEAD OF THE CALIPH. NOW, ON THE DAY WHEN OUR STORY BEGINS, THE VILE IZNOGOUD THOUGHT HE HAD FOUND A WAY TO ACHIEVE HIS OVERWEENING AMBITION...
THE CHALLENGE
I'VE GOT IT!
YES, WA'AT ALAHF, MY FAITHFUL STRONG-ARM MAN, I LOOKED IN THE BOOK OF LAWS AND I'VE FOUND A WAY TO BECOME CALIPH INSTEAD OF THE CALIPH!
OH, DROP IT, MASTER! YOU KNOW PERFECTLY WELL YOU ALWAYS LOSE IN THE END!
NOT THIS TIME. LISTEN: ARTICLE 312, PARAGRAPH A: ANY CITIZEN HAS THE RIGHT TO CHALLENGE THE CALIPH. HE MUST DO SO PUBLICLY AND USING THE FOLLOWING TERMS: "SCRAM, WATERMELON-HEAD*!" THE CALIPH CANNOT REFUSE TO FIGHT HIM.
*POTATOES DIDN'T EXIST IN BAGHDAD AT THIS TIME.
TEXT: GOSCINNY — DRAWING: TABARY —
... AND IF THE CALIPH IS DEFEATED IN ONE-ON-ONE COMBAT, HE IS INSTANTLY DEPOSED AND THE GRAND VIZIER BECOMES CALIPH!
I'M GOING TO BE CALIPH! I'M GOING TO BE CALIPH!
IT'S FUNNY THERE HAVEN'T EVER BEEN ANY CHALLENGES...
OH, THAT'S ON ACCOUNT OF PARAGRAPH B.
PARAGRAPH B?
IT STATES THAT THE VICTORIOUS CITIZEN IS TO BE BEHEADED FOR DARING TO HUMILIATE A CALIPH.
BUT NO ONE KNOWS ABOUT THIS LAW... SO LET'S GO AND FIND SOME SOLID, HEFTY CITIZEN. PREFERABLY A STUPID ONE.
AND WHERE ARE WE GOING TO FIND THIS SOLID CITIZEN?
IN THE FRUIT AND VEGETABLE MARKET OF KHO'VENTGHADEN, WHERE THE STRONGEST STREET PORTERS CAN BE FOUND.
1

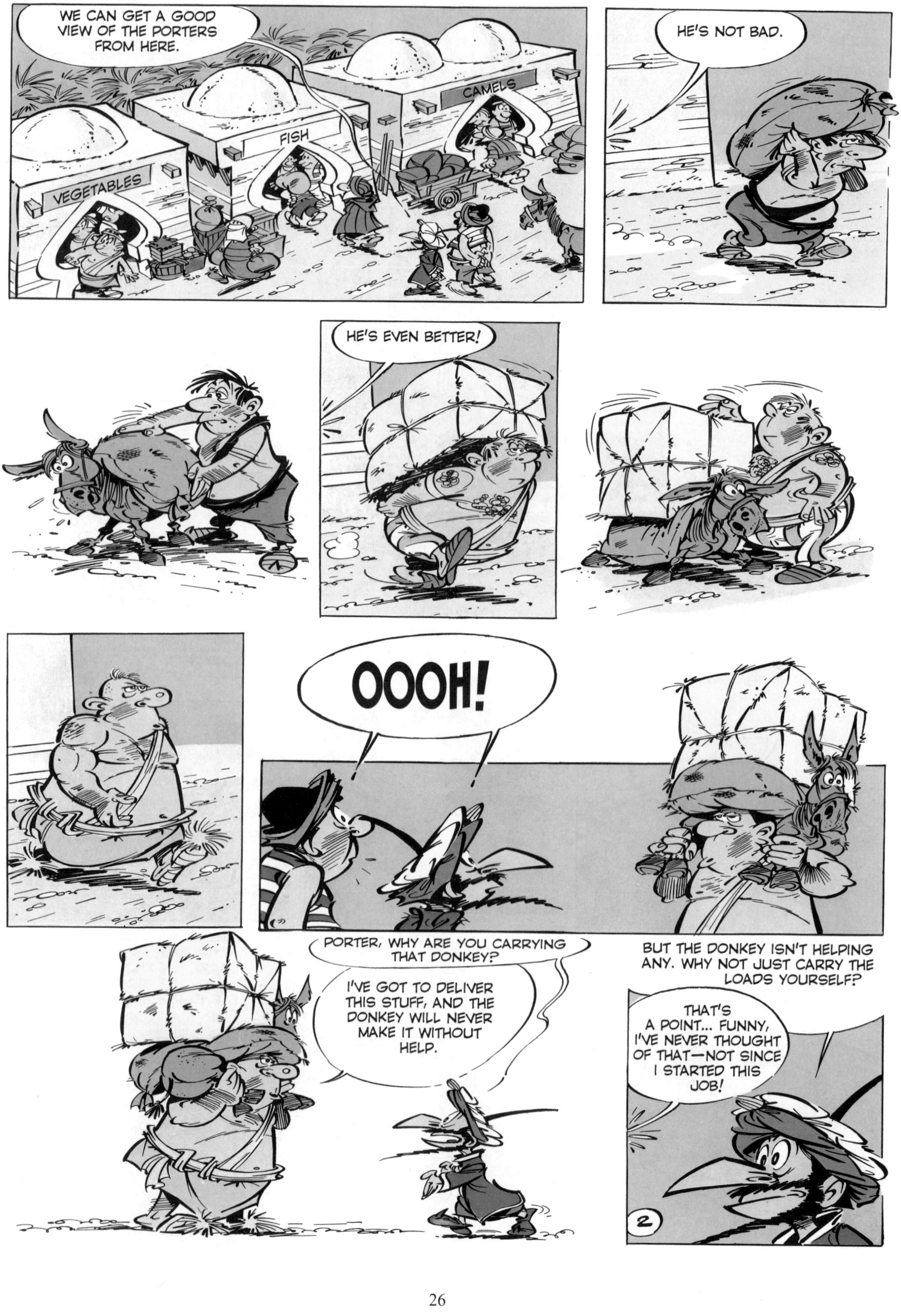
WE CAN GET A GOOD VIEW OF THE PORTERS FROM HERE.
CAMELS
FISH
VEGETABLES
HE'S NOT BAD.
HE'S EVEN BETTER!
OOOH!
PORTER, WHY ARE YOU CARRYING THAT DONKEY?
I'VE GOT TO DELIVER THIS STUFF, AND THE DONKEY WILL NEVER MAKE IT WITHOUT HELP.
BUT THE DONKEY ISN'T HELPING ANY. WHY NOT JUST CARRY THE LOADS YOURSELF?
THAT'S A POINT... FUNNY, I'VE NEVER THOUGHT OF THAT—NOT SINCE I STARTED THIS JOB!
2

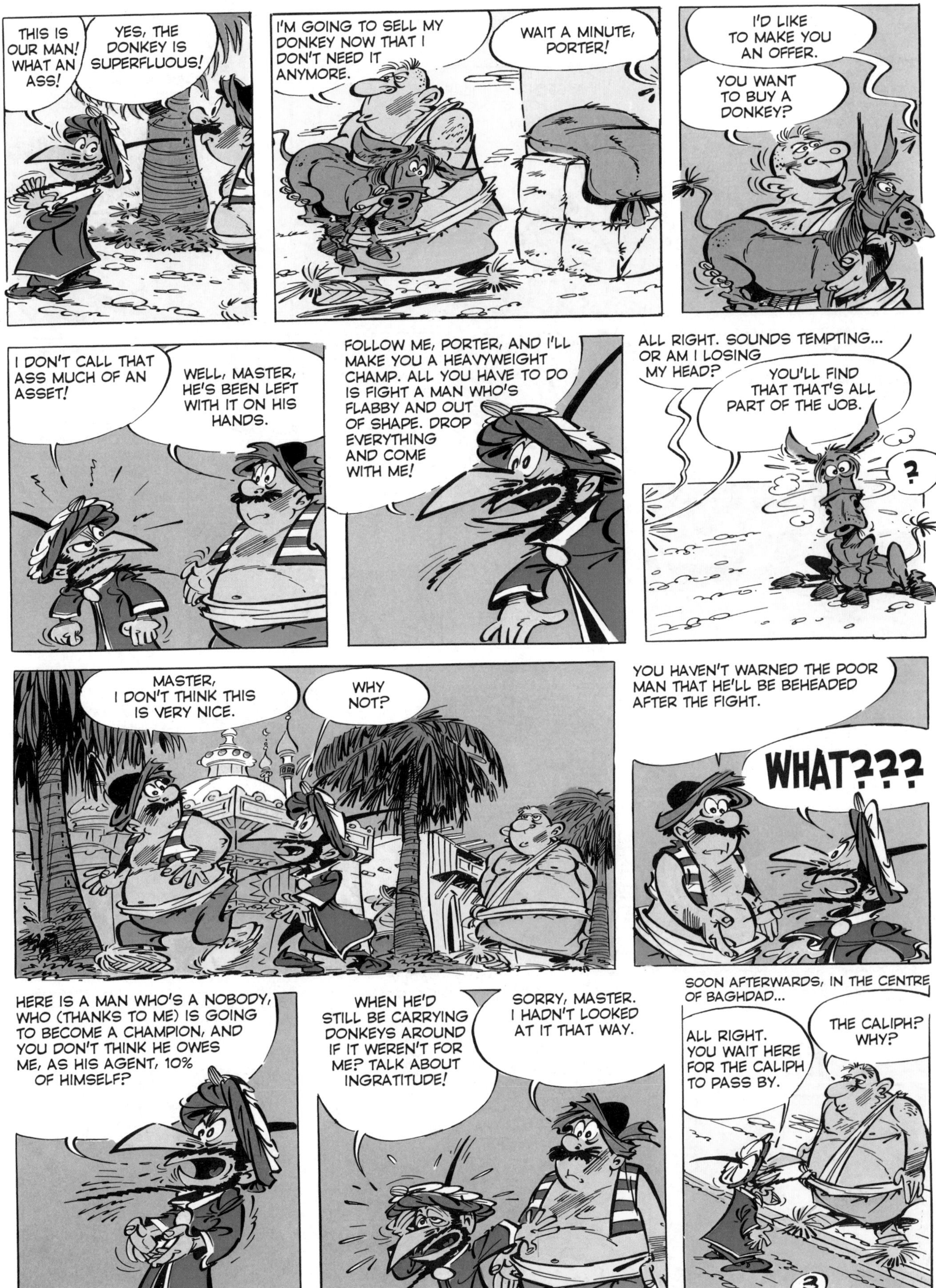

THIS IS OUR MAN! WHAT AN ASS!
YES, THE DONKEY IS SUPERFLUOUS!
I'M GOING TO SELL MY DONKEY NOW THAT I DON'T NEED IT ANYMORE.
WAIT A MINUTE, PORTER!
I'D LIKE TO MAKE YOU AN OFFER.
YOU WANT TO BUY A DONKEY?
I DON'T CALL THAT ASS MUCH OF AN ASSET!
WELL, MASTER, HE'S BEEN LEFT WITH IT ON HIS HANDS.
FOLLOW ME, PORTER, AND I'LL MAKE YOU A HEAVYWEIGHT CHAMP. ALL YOU HAVE TO DO IS FIGHT A MAN WHO'S FLABBY AND OUT OF SHAPE. DROP EVERYTHING AND COME WITH ME!
ALL RIGHT. SOUNDS TEMPTING... OR AM I LOSING MY HEAD?
YOU'LL FIND THAT THAT'S ALL PART OF THE JOB.
?
MASTER, I DON'T THINK THIS IS VERY NICE.
WHY NOT?
YOU HAVEN'T WARNED THE POOR MAN THAT HE'LL BE BEHEADED AFTER THE FIGHT.
WHAT???
HERE IS A MAN WHO'S A NOBODY, WHO (THANKS TO ME) IS GOING TO BECOME A CHAMPION, AND YOU DON'T THINK HE OWES ME, AS HIS AGENT, 10% OF HIMSELF?
WHEN HE'D STILL BE CARRYING DONKEYS AROUND IF IT WEREN'T FOR ME? TALK ABOUT INGRATITUDE!
SORRY, MASTER. I HADN'T LOOKED AT IT THAT WAY.
SOON AFTERWARDS, IN THE CENTRE OF BAGHDAD...
ALL RIGHT. YOU WAIT HERE FOR THE CALIPH TO PASS BY.
THE CALIPH? WHY?
3

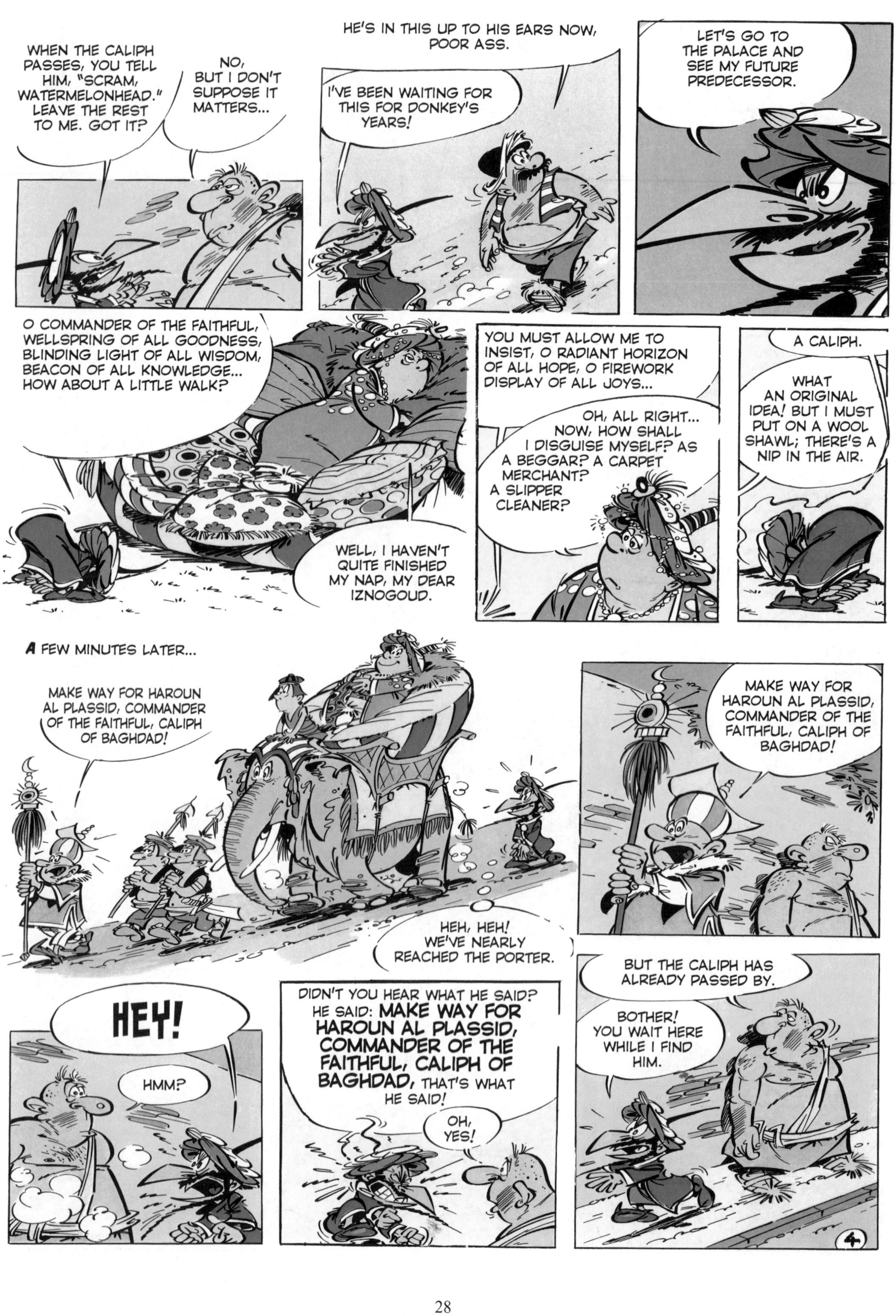

WHEN THE CALIPH PASSES, YOU TELL HIM, "SCRAM, WATERMELONHEAD." LEAVE THE REST TO ME. GOT IT?
NO, BUT I DON'T SUPPOSE IT MATTERS...
HE'S IN THIS UP TO HIS EARS NOW, POOR ASS.
I'VE BEEN WAITING FOR THIS FOR DONKEY'S YEARS!
LET'S GO TO THE PALACE AND SEE MY FUTURE PREDECESSOR.
O COMMANDER OF THE FAITHFUL, WELLSPRING OF ALL GOODNESS, BLINDING LIGHT OF ALL WISDOM, BEACON OF ALL KNOWLEDGE... HOW ABOUT A LITTLE WALK?
WELL, I HAVEN'T QUITE FINISHED MY NAP, MY DEAR IZNOGOUD.
YOU MUST ALLOW ME TO INSIST, O RADIANT HORIZON OF ALL HOPE, O FIREWORK DISPLAY OF ALL JOYS...
OH, ALL RIGHT... NOW, HOW SHALL I DISGUISE MYSELF? AS A BEGGAR? A CARPET MERCHANT? A SLIPPER CLEANER?
A CALIPH.
WHAT AN ORIGINAL IDEA! BUT I MUST PUT ON A WOOL SHAWL; THERE'S A NIP IN THE AIR.
A FEW MINUTES LATER...
MAKE WAY FOR HAROUN AL PLASSID, COMMANDER OF THE FAITHFUL, CALIPH OF BAGHDAD!
HEH, HEH! WE'VE NEARLY REACHED THE PORTER.
MAKE WAY FOR HAROUN AL PLASSID, COMMANDER OF THE FAITHFUL, CALIPH OF BAGHDAD!
HEY!
HMM?
DIDN'T YOU HEAR WHAT HE SAID? HE SAID: MAKE WAY FOR HAROUN AL PLASSID, COMMANDER OF THE FAITHFUL, CALIPH OF BAGHDAD, THAT'S WHAT HE SAID!
OH, YES!
BUT THE CALIPH HAS ALREADY PASSED BY.
BOTHER! YOU WAIT HERE WHILE I FIND HIM.
4

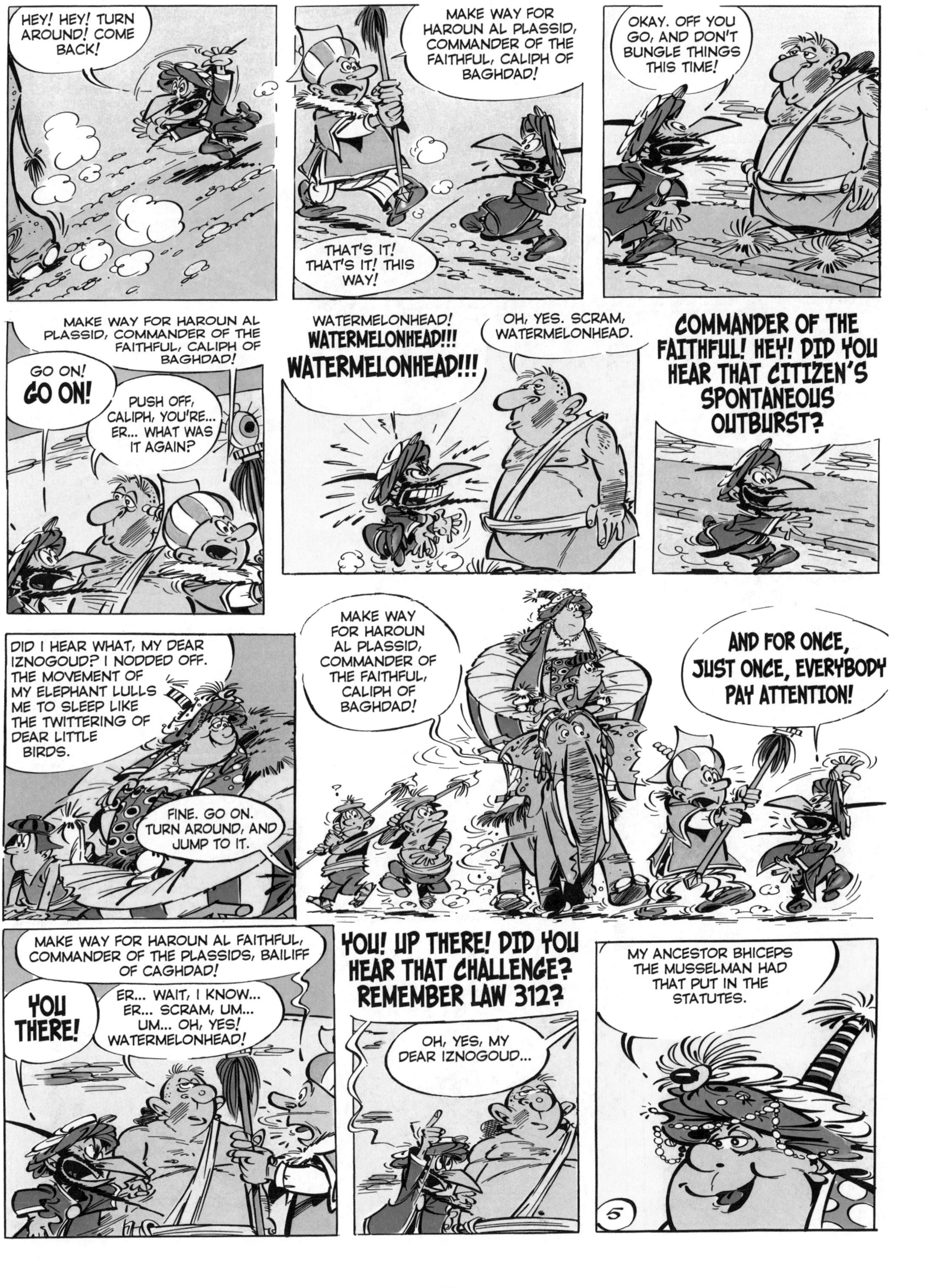
HEY! HEY! TURN AROUND! COME BACK!
MAKE WAY FOR HAROUN AL PLASSID, COMMANDER OF THE FAITHFUL, CALIPH OF BAGHDAD!
THAT'S IT! THAT'S IT! THIS WAY!
OKAY. OFF YOU GO, AND DON'T BUNGLE THINGS THIS TIME!
MAKE WAY FOR HAROUN AL PLASSID, COMMANDER OF THE FAITHFUL, CALIPH OF BAGHDAD!
GO ON! GO ON!
PUSH OFF, CALIPH, YOU'RE... ER... WHAT WAS IT AGAIN?
WATERMELONHEAD! WATERMELONHEAD!!! WATERMELONHEAD!!!
OH, YES. SCRAM, WATERMELONHEAD.
COMMANDER OF THE FAITHFUL! HEY! DID YOU HEAR THAT CITIZEN'S SPONTANEOUS OUTBURST?
DID I HEAR WHAT, MY DEAR IZNOGOUD? I NODDED OFF. THE MOVEMENT OF MY ELEPHANT LULLS ME TO SLEEP LIKE THE TWITTERING OF DEAR LITTLE BIRDS.
FINE. GO ON. TURN AROUND, AND JUMP TO IT.
MAKE WAY FOR HAROUN AL PLASSID, COMMANDER OF THE FAITHFUL, CALIPH OF BAGHDAD!
AND FOR ONCE, JUST ONCE, EVERYBODY PAY ATTENTION!
MAKE WAY FOR HAROUN AL FAITHFUL, COMMANDER OF THE PLASSIDS, BAILIFF OF CAGHDAD!
YOU THERE!
ER... WAIT, I KNOW... ER... SCRAM, UM... UM... OH, YES! WATERMELONHEAD!
YOU! UP THERE! DID YOU HEAR THAT CHALLENGE? REMEMBER LAW 312?
OH, YES, MY DEAR IZNOGOUD...
MY ANCESTOR BHICEPS THE MUSSELMAN HAD THAT PUT IN THE STATUTES.
5

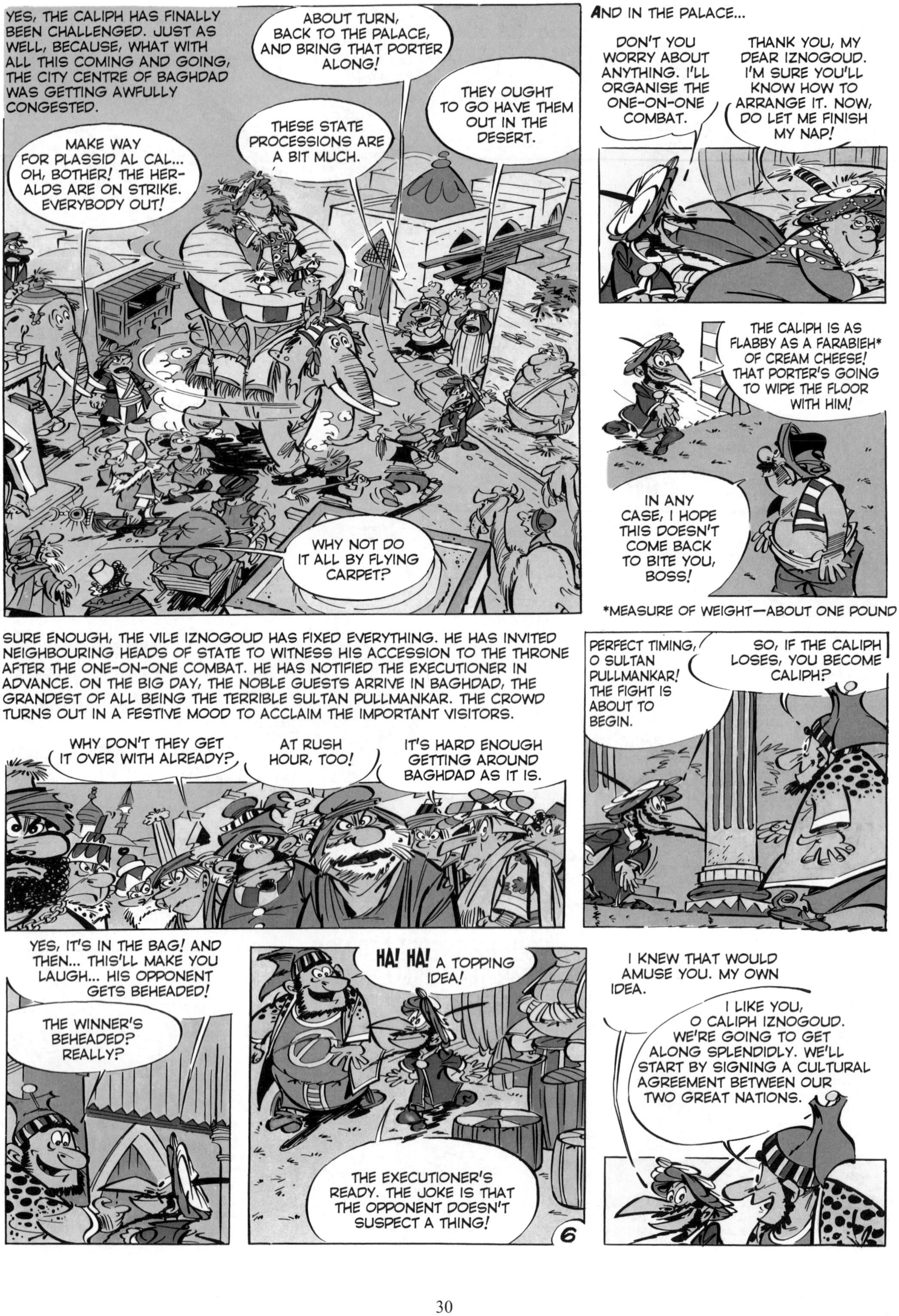
YES, THE CALIPH HAS FINALLY BEEN CHALLENGED. JUST AS WELL, BECAUSE, WHAT WITH ALL THIS COMING AND GOING, THE CITY CENTRE OF BAGHDAD WAS GETTING AWFULLY CONGESTED.
ABOUT TURN, BACK TO THE PALACE, AND BRING THAT PORTER ALONG!
THEY OUGHT TO GO HAVE THEM OUT IN THE DESERT.
THESE STATE PROCESSIONS ARE A BIT MUCH.
MAKE WAY FOR PLASSID AL CAL... OH, BOTHER! THE HER-ALDS ARE ON STRIKE. EVERYBODY OUT!
WHY NOT DO IT ALL BY FLYING CARPET?
AND IN THE PALACE...
DON'T YOU WORRY ABOUT ANYTHING. I'LL ORGANISE THE ONE-ON-ONE COMBAT.
THANK YOU, MY DEAR IZNOGOUD. I'M SURE YOU'LL KNOW HOW TO ARRANGE IT. NOW, DO LET ME FINISH MY NAP!
THE CALIPH IS AS FLABBY AS A FARABIEH* OF CREAM CHEESE! THAT PORTER'S GOING TO WIPE THE FLOOR WITH HIM!
IN ANY CASE, I HOPE THIS DOESN'T COME BACK TO BITE YOU, BOSS!
*MEASURE OF WEIGHT—ABOUT ONE POUND
SURE ENOUGH, THE VILE IZNOGOUD HAS FIXED EVERYTHING. HE HAS INVITED NEIGHBOURING HEADS OF STATE TO WITNESS HIS ACCESSION TO THE THRONE AFTER THE ONE-ON-ONE COMBAT. HE HAS NOTIFIED THE EXECUTIONER IN ADVANCE. ON THE BIG DAY, THE NOBLE GUESTS ARRIVE IN BAGHDAD, THE GRANDEST OF ALL BEING THE TERRIBLE SULTAN PULLMANKAR. THE CROWD TURNS OUT IN A FESTIVE MOOD TO ACCLAIM THE IMPORTANT VISITORS.
WHY DON'T THEY GET IT OVER WITH ALREADY?
AT RUSH HOUR, TOO!
IT'S HARD ENOUGH GETTING AROUND BAGHDAD AS IT IS.
PERFECT TIMING, O SULTAN PULLMANKAR! THE FIGHT IS ABOUT TO BEGIN.
SO, IF THE CALIPH LOSES, YOU BECOME CALIPH?
YES, IT'S IN THE BAG! AND THEN... THIS'LL MAKE YOU LAUGH... HIS OPPONENT GETS BEHEADED!
THE WINNER'S BEHEADED? REALLY?
HA! HA! A TOPPING IDEA!
THE EXECUTIONER'S READY. THE JOKE IS THAT THE OPPONENT DOESN'T SUSPECT A THING!
6
I KNEW THAT WOULD AMUSE YOU. MY OWN IDEA.
I LIKE YOU, O CALIPH IZNOGOUD. WE'RE GOING TO GET ALONG SPLENDIDLY. WE'LL START BY SIGNING A CULTURAL AGREEMENT BETWEEN OUR TWO GREAT NATIONS.

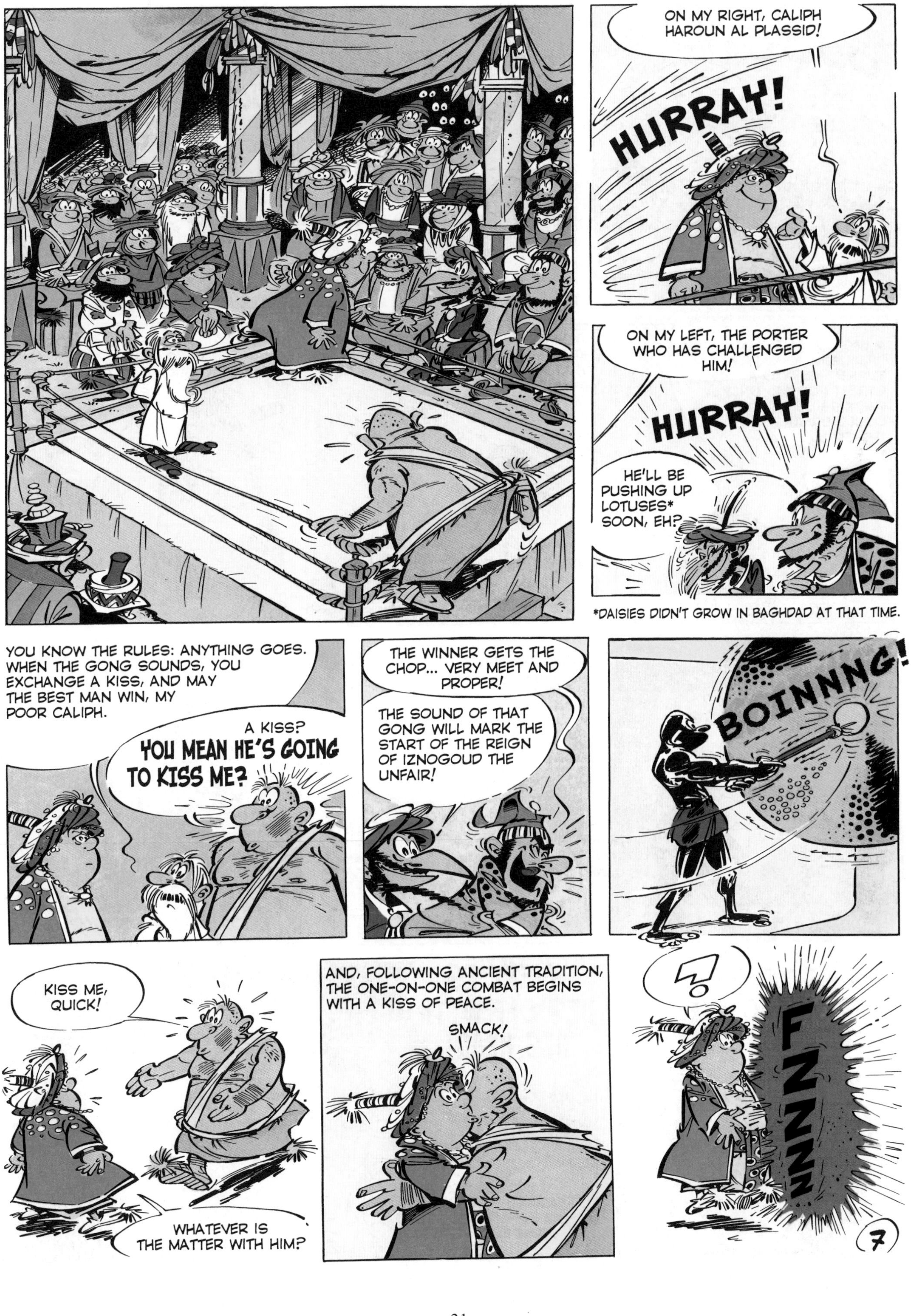
ON MY RIGHT, CALIPH HAROUN AL PLASSID!
HURRAY!
ON MY LEFT, THE PORTER WHO HAS CHALLENGED HIM!
HURRAY!
HE'LL BE PUSHING UP LOTUSES* SOON, EH?
*DAISIES DIDN'T GROW IN BAGHDAD AT THAT TIME.
YOU KNOW THE RULES: ANYTHING GOES. WHEN THE GONG SOUNDS, YOU EXCHANGE A KISS, AND MAY THE BEST MAN WIN, MY POOR CALIPH.
A KISS? YOU MEAN HE'S GOING TO KISS ME?
THE WINNER GETS THE CHOP... VERY MEET AND PROPER!
THE SOUND OF THAT GONG WILL MARK THE START OF THE REIGN OF IZNOGOUD THE UNFAIR!
BOINNNG!
KISS ME, QUICK!
WHATEVER IS THE MATTER WITH HIM?
AND, FOLLOWING ANCIENT TRADITION, THE ONE-ON-ONE COMBAT BEGINS WITH A KISS OF PEACE.
SMACK!
?
FZZZZ
7

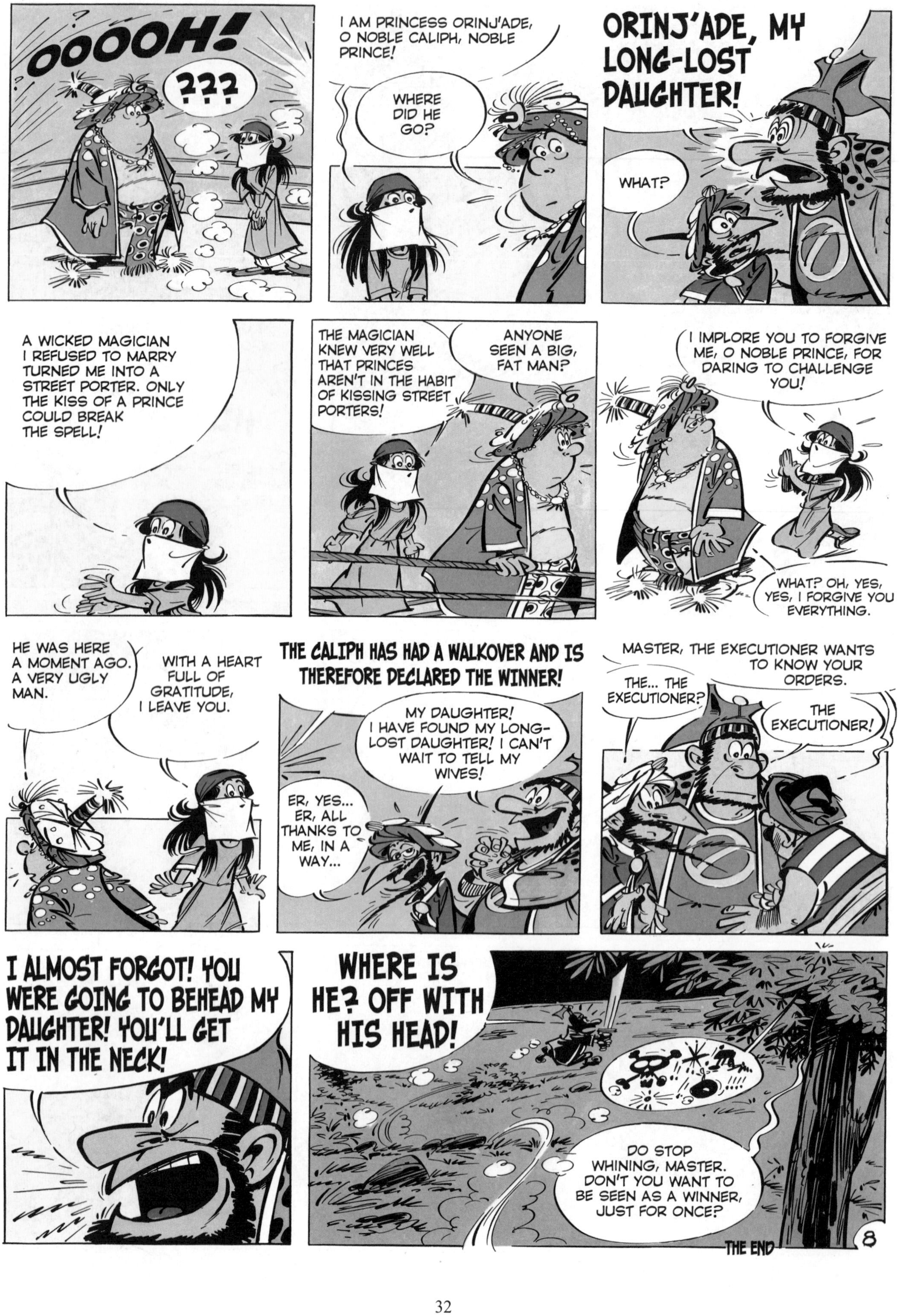
OOOOH!
???
I AM PRINCESS ORINJ'ADE, O NOBLE CALIPH, NOBLE PRINCE!
WHERE DID HE GO?
ORINJ'ADE, MY LONG-LOST DAUGHTER!
WHAT?
A WICKED MAGICIAN I REFUSED TO MARRY TURNED ME INTO A STREET PORTER. ONLY THE KISS OF A PRINCE COULD BREAK THE SPELL!
THE MAGICIAN KNEW VERY WELL THAT PRINCES AREN'T IN THE HABIT OF KISSING STREET PORTERS!
ANYONE SEEN A BIG, FAT MAN?
I IMPLORE YOU TO FORGIVE ME, O NOBLE PRINCE, FOR DARING TO CHALLENGE YOU!
WHAT? OH, YES, YES, I FORGIVE YOU EVERYTHING.
HE WAS HERE A MOMENT AGO. A VERY UGLY MAN.
WITH A HEART FULL OF GRATITUDE, I LEAVE YOU.
THE CALIPH HAS HAD A WALKOVER AND IS THEREFORE DECLARED THE WINNER!
MY DAUGHTER! I HAVE FOUND MY LONG-LOST DAUGHTER! I CAN'T WAIT TO TELL MY WIVES!
ER, YES... ER, ALL THANKS TO ME, IN A WAY...
MASTER, THE EXECUTIONER WANTS TO KNOW YOUR ORDERS.
THE... THE EXECUTIONER?
THE EXECUTIONER!
I ALMOST FORGOT! YOU WERE GOING TO BEHEAD MY DAUGHTER! YOU'LL GET IT IN THE NECK!
WHERE IS HE? OFF WITH HIS HEAD!
DO STOP WHINING, MASTER. DON'T YOU WANT TO BE SEEN AS A WINNER, JUST FOR ONCE?
THE END
8

THE LABYRINTH

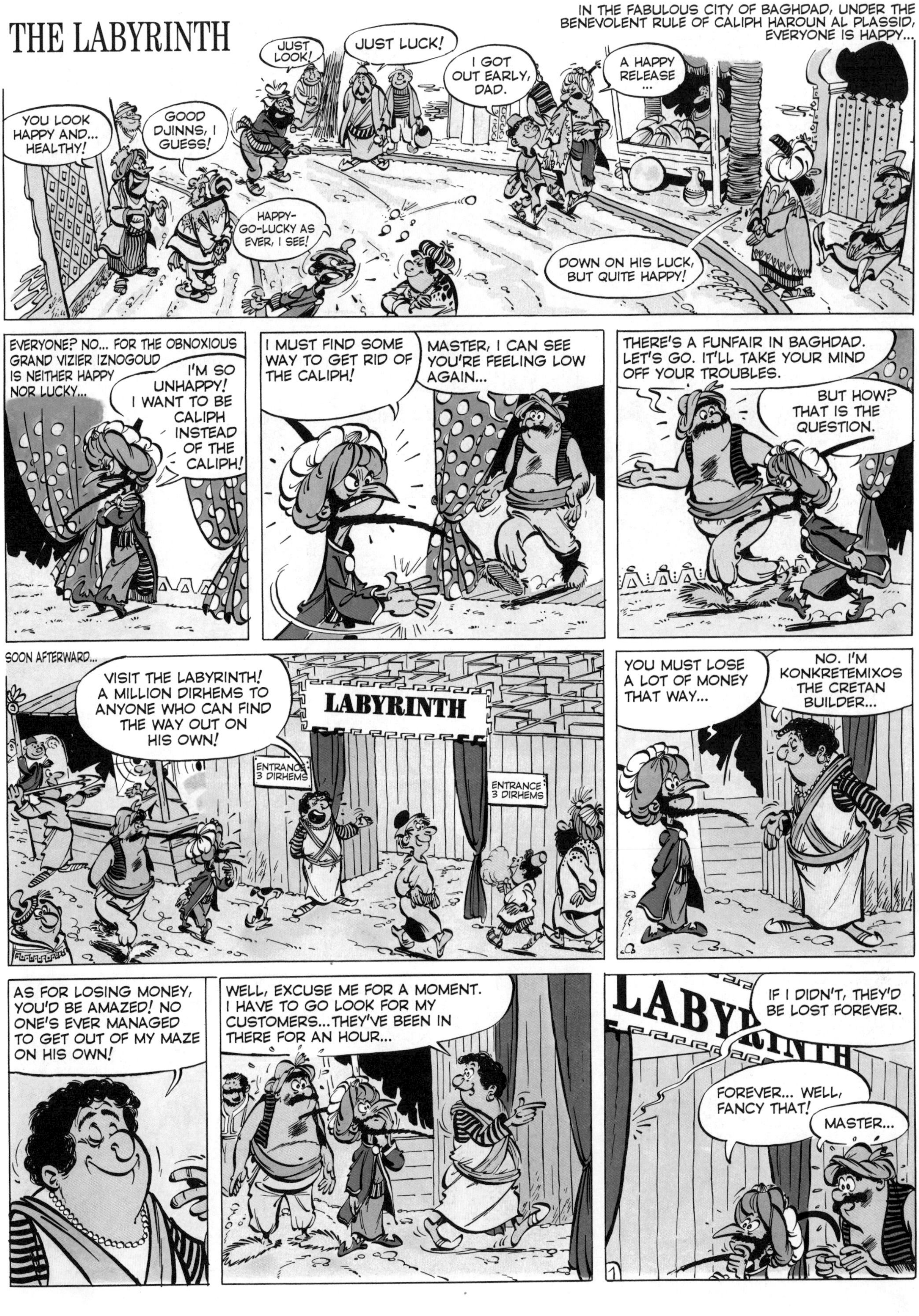
IN THE FABULOUS CITY OF BAGHDAD, UNDER THE BENEVOLENT RULE OF CALIPH HAROUN AL PLASSID, EVERYONE IS HAPPY...
YOU LOOK HAPPY AND... HEALTHY!
GOOD DJINNS, I GUESS!
JUST LOOK!
JUST LUCK!
HAPPY-GO-LUCKY AS EVER, I SEE!
I GOT OUT EARLY, DAD.
A HAPPY RELEASE ...
DOWN ON HIS LUCK, BUT QUITE HAPPY!
EVERYONE? NO... FOR THE OBNOXIOUS GRAND VIZIER IZNOGOUD IS NEITHER HAPPY NOR LUCKY...
I'M SO UNHAPPY! I WANT TO BE CALIPH INSTEAD OF THE CALIPH!
I MUST FIND SOME WAY TO GET RID OF THE CALIPH!
MASTER, I CAN SEE YOU'RE FEELING LOW AGAIN...
THERE'S A FUNFAIR IN BAGHDAD. LET'S GO. IT'LL TAKE YOUR MIND OFF YOUR TROUBLES.
BUT HOW? THAT IS THE QUESTION.
SOON AFTERWARD...
VISIT THE LABYRINTH! A MILLION DIRHEMS TO ANYONE WHO CAN FIND THE WAY OUT ON HIS OWN!
LABYRINTH
ENTRANCE 3 DIRHEMS
ENTRANCE 3 DIRHEMS
YOU MUST LOSE A LOT OF MONEY THAT WAY...
NO. I'M KONKRETEMIXOS THE CRETAN BUILDER...
AS FOR LOSING MONEY, YOU'D BE AMAZED! NO ONE'S EVER MANAGED TO GET OUT OF MY MAZE ON HIS OWN!
WELL, EXCUSE ME FOR A MOMENT. I HAVE TO GO LOOK FOR MY CUSTOMERS...THEY'VE BEEN IN THERE FOR AN HOUR...
LABYRINTH
IF I DIDN'T, THEY'D BE LOST FOREVER.
FOREVER... WELL, FANCY THAT!
MASTER...

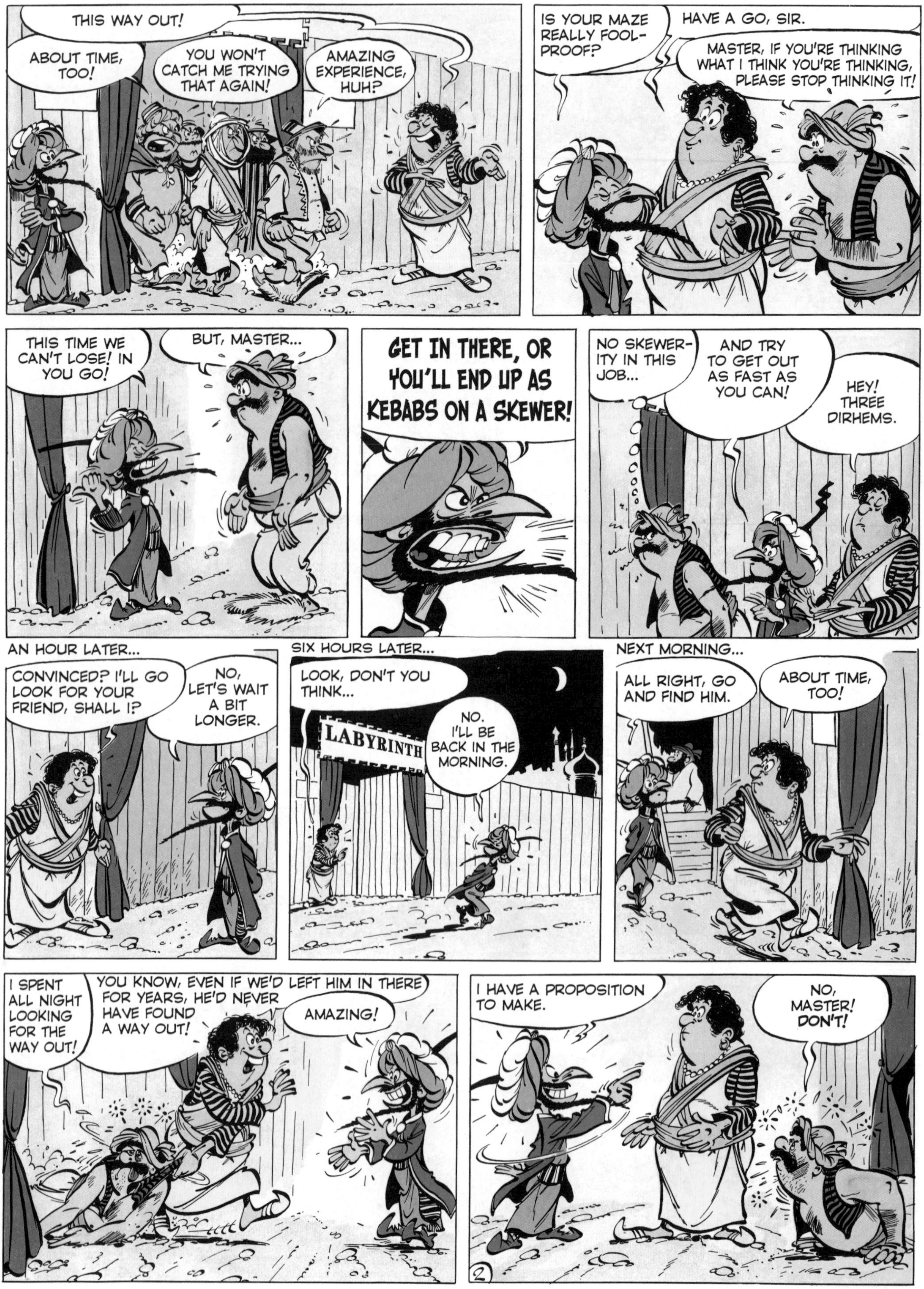
THIS WAY OUT!
ABOUT TIME, TOO!
YOU WON'T CATCH ME TRYING THAT AGAIN!
AMAZING EXPERIENCE, HUH?
IS YOUR MAZE REALLY FOOL-PROOF?
HAVE A GO, SIR.
MASTER, IF YOU'RE THINKING WHAT I THINK YOU'RE THINKING, PLEASE STOP THINKING IT!
THIS TIME WE CAN'T LOSE! IN YOU GO!
BUT, MASTER...
GET IN THERE, OR YOU'LL END UP AS KEBABS ON A SKEWER!
NO SKEWER-ITY IN THIS JOB...
AND TRY TO GET OUT AS FAST AS YOU CAN!
HEY! THREE DIRHEMS.
AN HOUR LATER...
CONVINCED? I'LL GO LOOK FOR YOUR FRIEND, SHALL I?
NO, LET'S WAIT A BIT LONGER.
SIX HOURS LATER...
LOOK, DON'T YOU THINK...
LABYRINTH
NO. I'LL BE BACK IN THE MORNING.
NEXT MORNING...
ALL RIGHT, GO AND FIND HIM.
ABOUT TIME, TOO!
I SPENT ALL NIGHT LOOKING FOR THE WAY OUT!
YOU KNOW, EVEN IF WE'D LEFT HIM IN THERE FOR YEARS, HE'D NEVER HAVE FOUND A WAY OUT!
AMAZING!
I HAVE A PROPOSITION TO MAKE.
NO, MASTER! DON'T!

SELL MY LABYRINTH? NOT FOR 50,000 PIASTRES!

50,000 PIASTRES AND ONE DIRHEM.

SOLD!

FINE. COME AND SET UP YOUR LABYRINTH ON THE PALACE GROUNDS TOMORROW AT DAWN.

NEXT MORNING, HALF AN HOUR AFTER DAWN...

I'M A BIT LATE. I TOOK A WRONG TURN. I'M LOST OUTSIDE MY LABYRINTH.

GET TO WORK!

LATER...

HE'S TAKING HIS TIME.

MASTER, DROP THE IDEA!

BANG BANG
BANG BANG

LABYRINTH

GO TELL HIM TO HURRY UP!

ALL RIGHT, MASTER. BUT I GET THE FEELING YOU'RE GOING TO LOSE WITH THIS LABYRINTH.

WA'AT ALAHF'S BEEN GONE FOR AN HOUR. WHAT ARE THEY UP?

THAT'S IT. WHERE'S MY MONEY?

AT LAST!

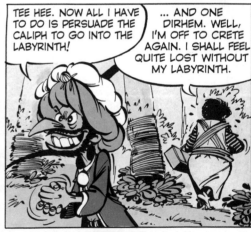

TEE HEE. NOW ALL I HAVE TO DO IS PERSUADE THE CALIPH TO GO INTO THE LABYRINTH!

... AND ONE DIRHEM. WELL, I'M OFF TO CRETE AGAIN. I SHALL FEEL QUITE LOST WITHOUT MY LABYRINTH.

WHERE'S WA'AT ALAHF? I FORGOT ABOUT HIM... OH, WELL. I MUST GO AND FIND THE CALIPH.

GOOD CALIPH HAROUN AL PLASSID, UNAWARE OF THE LABYRINTHINE PLOT BEING HATCHED, IS IN CONFERENCE WITH HIS MASTER OF GAMES...

THREE SULTANS!

I ONLY HAVE TWO VIZIERS, COMMANDER OF THE FAITHFUL.

③

35

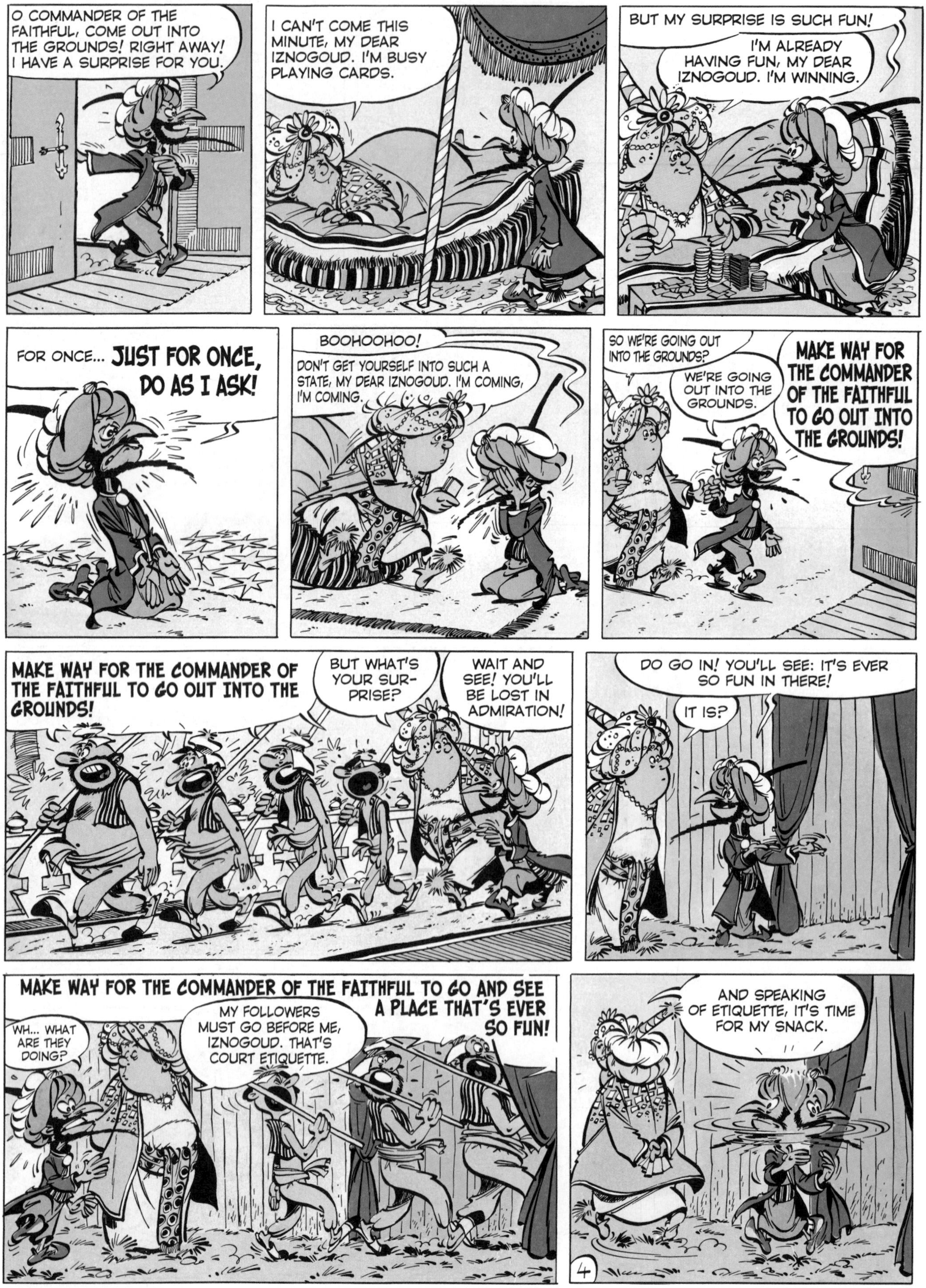

O COMMANDER OF THE FAITHFUL, COME OUT INTO THE GROUNDS! RIGHT AWAY! I HAVE A SURPRISE FOR YOU.
I CAN'T COME THIS MINUTE, MY DEAR IZNOGOUD. I'M BUSY PLAYING CARDS.
BUT MY SURPRISE IS SUCH FUN!
I'M ALREADY HAVING FUN, MY DEAR IZNOGOUD. I'M WINNING.
FOR ONCE... JUST FOR ONCE, DO AS I ASK!
BOOHOOHOO!
DON'T GET YOURSELF INTO SUCH A STATE, MY DEAR IZNOGOUD. I'M COMING, I'M COMING.
SO WE'RE GOING OUT INTO THE GROUNDS?
WE'RE GOING OUT INTO THE GROUNDS.
MAKE WAY FOR THE COMMANDER OF THE FAITHFUL TO GO OUT INTO THE GROUNDS!
MAKE WAY FOR THE COMMANDER OF THE FAITHFUL TO GO OUT INTO THE GROUNDS!
BUT WHAT'S YOUR SURPRISE?
WAIT AND SEE! YOU'LL BE LOST IN ADMIRATION!
DO GO IN! YOU'LL SEE: IT'S EVER SO FUN IN THERE!
IT IS?
MAKE WAY FOR THE COMMANDER OF THE FAITHFUL TO GO AND SEE A PLACE THAT'S EVER SO FUN!
WH... WHAT ARE THEY DOING?
MY FOLLOWERS MUST GO BEFORE ME, IZNOGOUD. THAT'S COURT ETIQUETTE.
AND SPEAKING OF ETIQUETTE, IT'S TIME FOR MY SNACK.
4

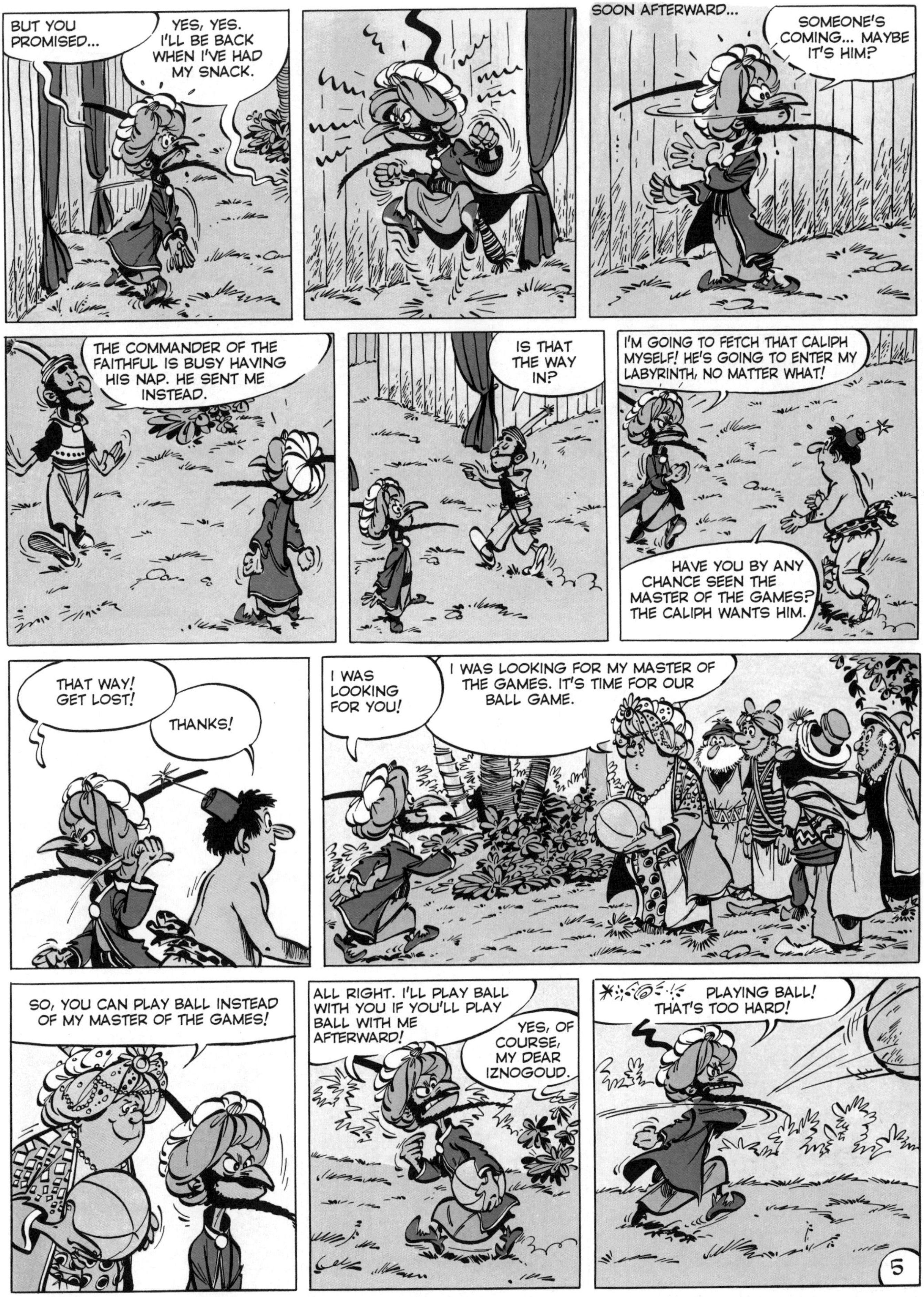
BUT YOU PROMISED...
YES, YES. I'LL BE BACK WHEN I'VE HAD MY SNACK.
SOON AFTERWARD...
SOMEONE'S COMING... MAYBE IT'S HIM?
THE COMMANDER OF THE FAITHFUL IS BUSY HAVING HIS NAP. HE SENT ME INSTEAD.
IS THAT THE WAY IN?
I'M GOING TO FETCH THAT CALIPH MYSELF! HE'S GOING TO ENTER MY LABYRINTH, NO MATTER WHAT!
HAVE YOU BY ANY CHANCE SEEN THE MASTER OF THE GAMES? THE CALIPH WANTS HIM.
THAT WAY! GET LOST!
THANKS!
I WAS LOOKING FOR YOU!
I WAS LOOKING FOR MY MASTER OF THE GAMES. IT'S TIME FOR OUR BALL GAME.
SO, YOU CAN PLAY BALL INSTEAD OF MY MASTER OF THE GAMES!
ALL RIGHT. I'LL PLAY BALL WITH YOU IF YOU'LL PLAY BALL WITH ME AFTERWARD!
YES, OF COURSE, MY DEAR IZNOGOUD.
PLAYING BALL! THAT'S TOO HARD!
5

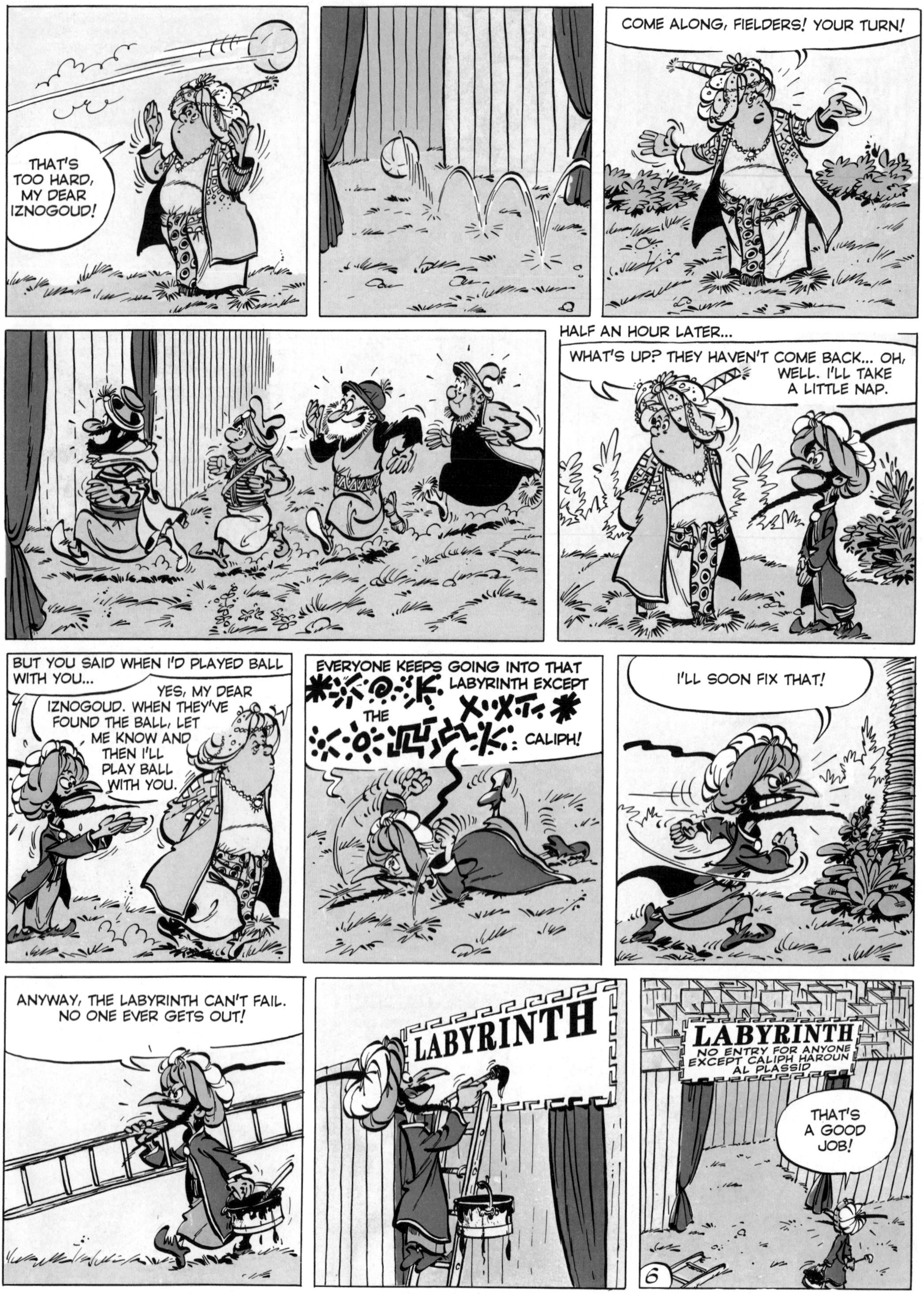
THAT'S TOO HARD, MY DEAR IZNOGOUD!
COME ALONG, FIELDERS! YOUR TURN!
HALF AN HOUR LATER...
WHAT'S UP? THEY HAVEN'T COME BACK... OH, WELL. I'LL TAKE A LITTLE NAP.
BUT YOU SAID WHEN I'D PLAYED BALL WITH YOU...
YES, MY DEAR IZNOGOUD. WHEN THEY'VE FOUND THE BALL, LET ME KNOW AND THEN I'LL PLAY BALL WITH YOU.
EVERYONE KEEPS GOING INTO THAT LABYRINTH EXCEPT THE CALIPH!
I'LL SOON FIX THAT!
ANYWAY, THE LABYRINTH CAN'T FAIL. NO ONE EVER GETS OUT!
LABYRINTH
LABYRINTH
NO ENTRY FOR ANYONE EXCEPT CALIPH HAROUN AL PLASSID
THAT'S A GOOD JOB!
6

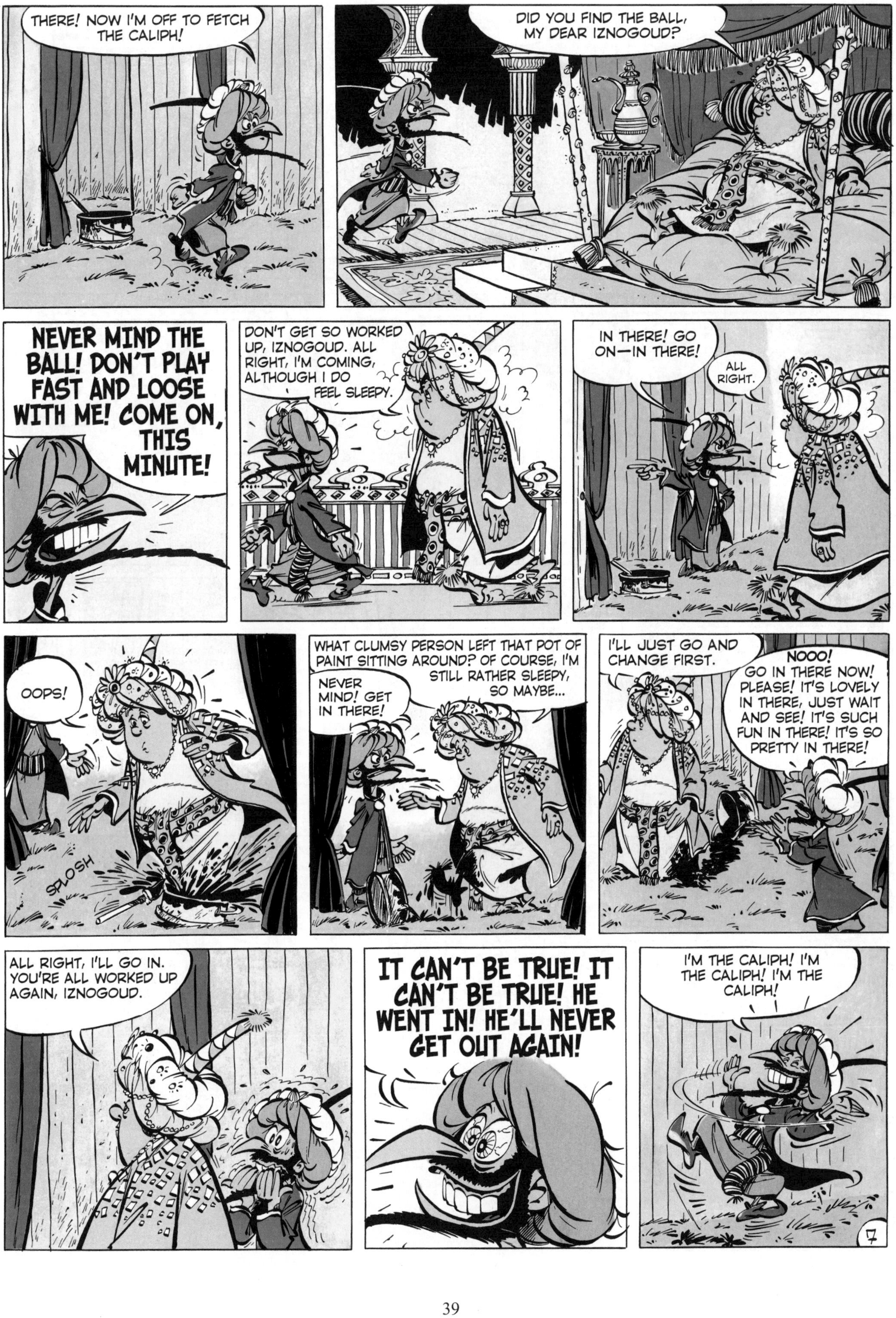
THERE! NOW I'M OFF TO FETCH THE CALIPH!
DID YOU FIND THE BALL, MY DEAR IZNOGOUD?
NEVER MIND THE BALL! DON'T PLAY FAST AND LOOSE WITH ME! COME ON, THIS MINUTE!
DON'T GET SO WORKED UP, IZNOGOUD. ALL RIGHT, I'M COMING, ALTHOUGH I DO FEEL SLEEPY.
IN THERE! GO ON—IN THERE!
ALL RIGHT.
OOPS!
SPLOSH
WHAT CLUMSY PERSON LEFT THAT POT OF PAINT SITTING AROUND? OF COURSE, I'M STILL RATHER SLEEPY, SO MAYBE...
NEVER MIND! GET IN THERE!
I'LL JUST GO AND CHANGE FIRST.
NOOO! GO IN THERE NOW! PLEASE! IT'S LOVELY IN THERE, JUST WAIT AND SEE! IT'S SUCH FUN IN THERE! IT'S SO PRETTY IN THERE!
ALL RIGHT, I'LL GO IN. YOU'RE ALL WORKED UP AGAIN, IZNOGOUD.
IT CAN'T BE TRUE! IT CAN'T BE TRUE! HE WENT IN! HE'LL NEVER GET OUT AGAIN!
I'M THE CALIPH! I'M THE CALIPH! I'M THE CALIPH!
7

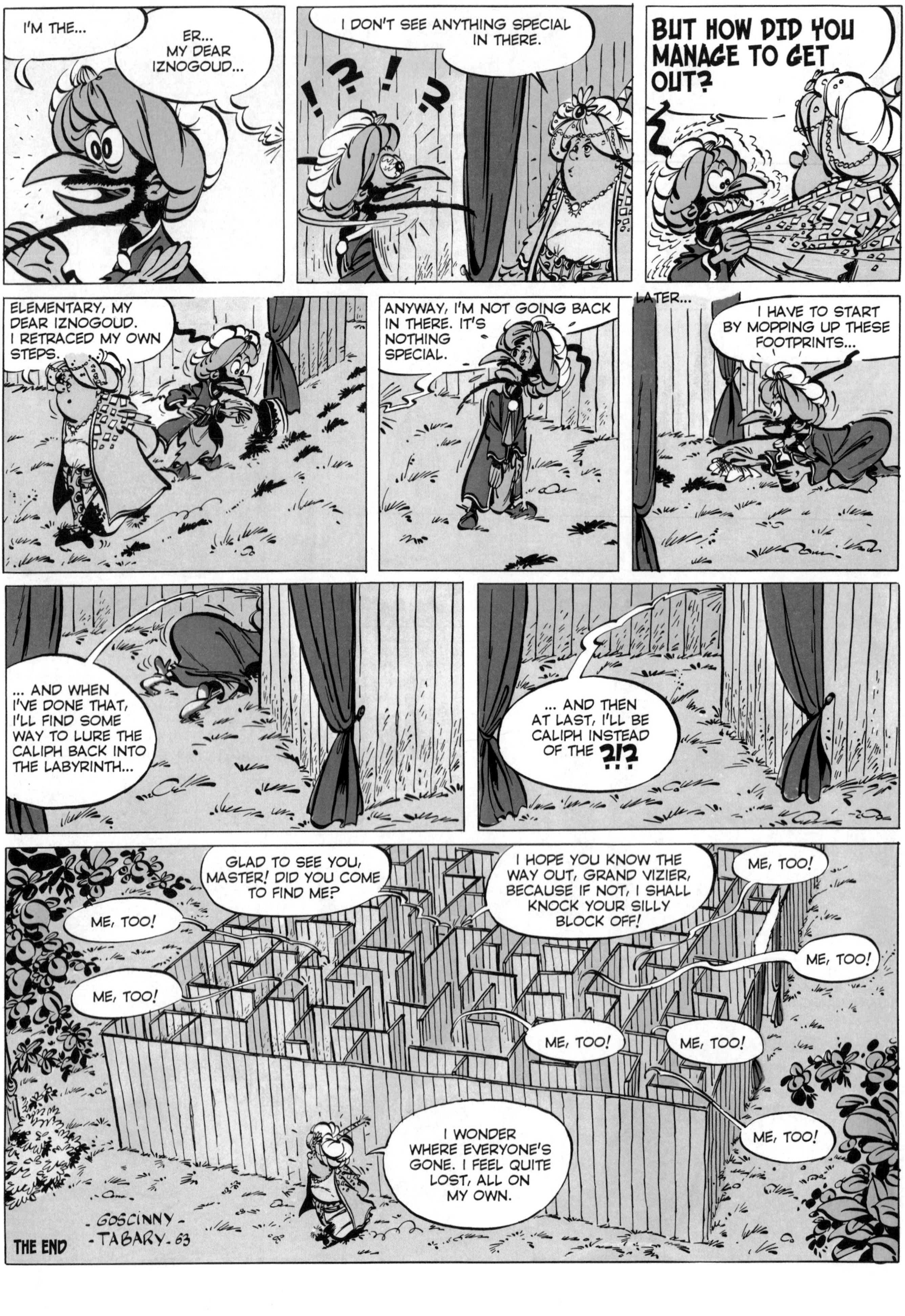
I'M THE...
ER... MY DEAR IZNOGOUD...
I DON'T SEE ANYTHING SPECIAL IN THERE.
!?!?
BUT HOW DID YOU MANAGE TO GET OUT?
ELEMENTARY, MY DEAR IZNOGOUD. I RETRACED MY OWN STEPS.
ANYWAY, I'M NOT GOING BACK IN THERE. IT'S NOTHING SPECIAL.
LATER...
I HAVE TO START BY MOPPING UP THESE FOOTPRINTS...
... AND WHEN I'VE DONE THAT, I'LL FIND SOME WAY TO LURE THE CALIPH BACK INTO THE LABYRINTH...
... AND THEN AT LAST, I'LL BE CALIPH INSTEAD OF THE ?!?
GLAD TO SEE YOU, MASTER! DID YOU COME TO FIND ME?
I HOPE YOU KNOW THE WAY OUT, GRAND VIZIER, BECAUSE IF NOT, I SHALL KNOCK YOUR SILLY BLOCK OFF!
ME, TOO!
ME, TOO!
ME, TOO!
ME, TOO!
ME, TOO!
ME, TOO!
ME, TOO!
I WONDER WHERE EVERYONE'S GONE. I FEEL QUITE LOST, ALL ON MY OWN.
-GOSCINNY-
-TABARY-63
THE END

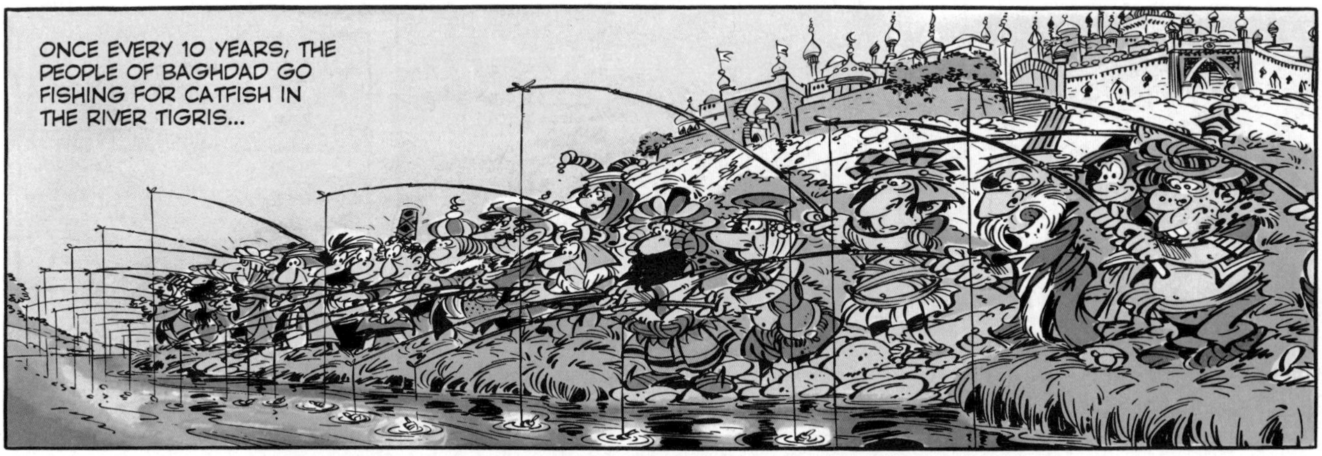
ONCE EVERY 10 YEARS, THE PEOPLE OF BAGHDAD GO FISHING FOR CATFISH IN THE RIVER TIGRIS...

WHY? BECAUSE ONCE EVERY 10 YEARS, THEY HOLD...

ELECTIONS IN THE CALIPHATE

TEXT: GOSCINNY

DRAWING: TABARY-72

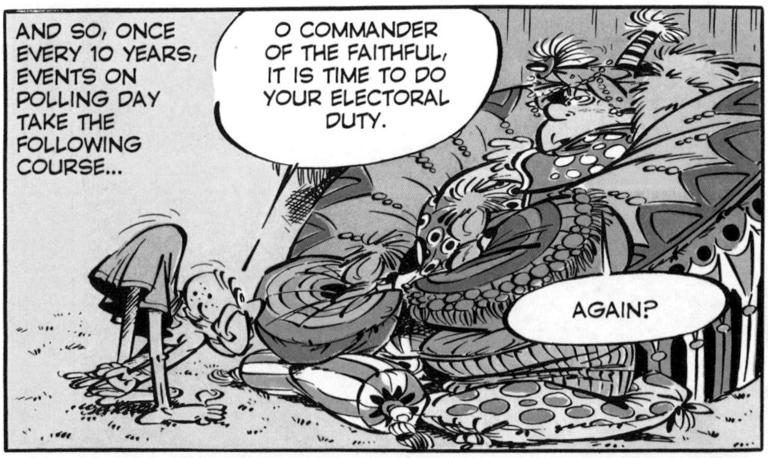
AND SO, ONCE EVERY 10 YEARS, EVENTS ON POLLING DAY TAKE THE FOLLOWING COURSE...
O COMMANDER OF THE FAITHFUL, IT IS TIME TO DO YOUR ELECTORAL DUTY.
AGAIN?

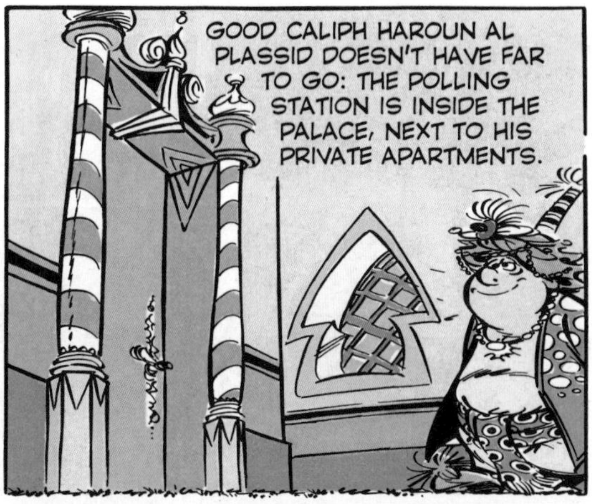
GOOD CALIPH HAROUN AL PLASSID DOESN'T HAVE FAR TO GO: THE POLLING STATION IS INSIDE THE PALACE, NEXT TO HIS PRIVATE APARTMENTS.

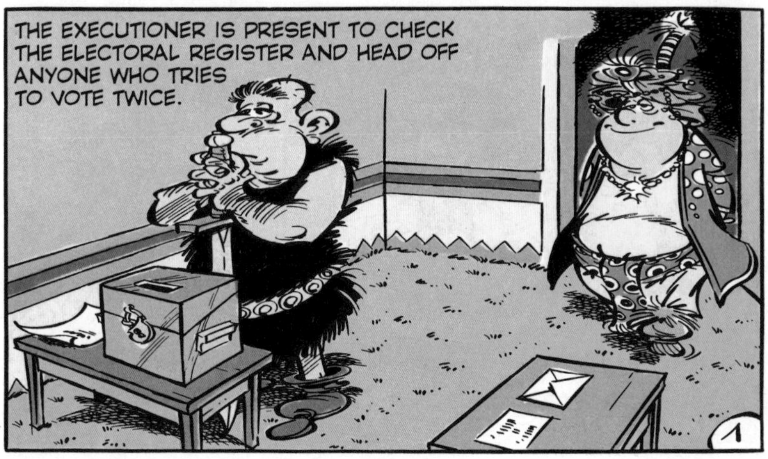
THE EXECUTIONER IS PRESENT TO CHECK THE ELECTORAL REGISTER AND HEAD OFF ANYONE WHO TRIES TO VOTE TWICE.
1

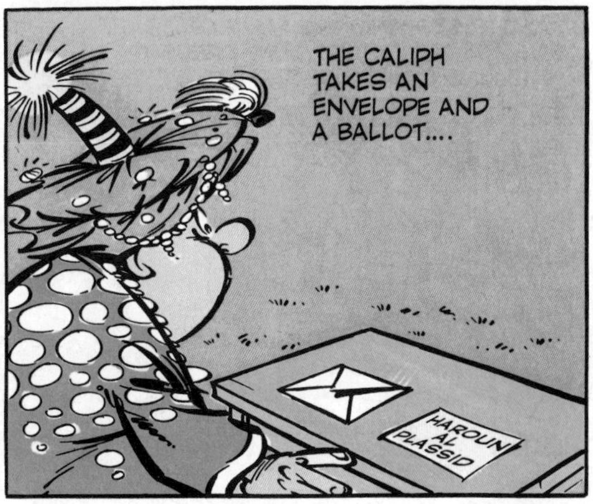
THE CALIPH TAKES AN ENVELOPE AND A BALLOT....
HAROUN AL PLASSID

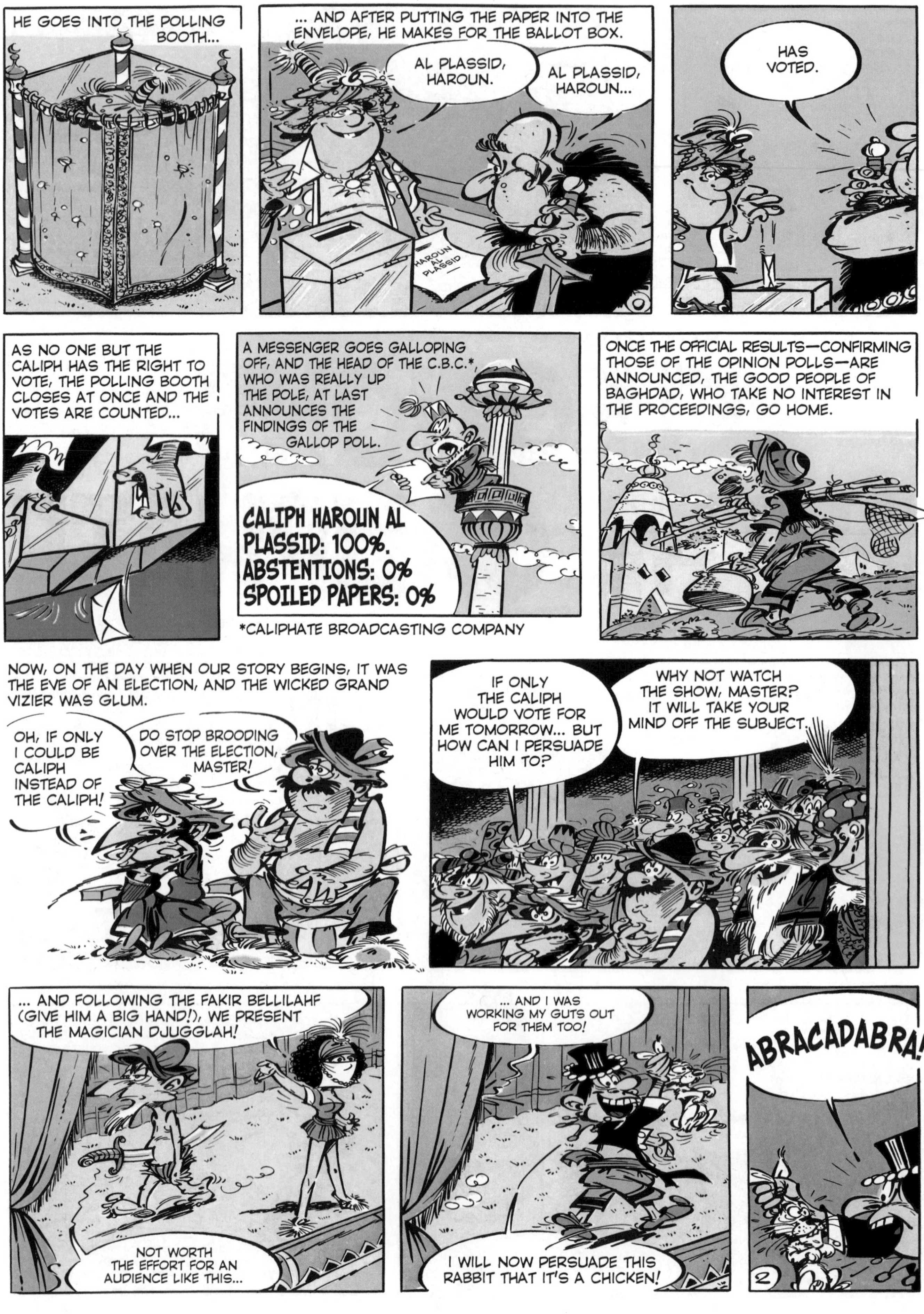
HE GOES INTO THE POLLING BOOTH...
... AND AFTER PUTTING THE PAPER INTO THE ENVELOPE, HE MAKES FOR THE BALLOT BOX.
AL PLASSID, HAROUN.
AL PLASSID, HAROUN...
HAROUN AL PLASSID
HAS VOTED.
AS NO ONE BUT THE CALIPH HAS THE RIGHT TO VOTE, THE POLLING BOOTH CLOSES AT ONCE AND THE VOTES ARE COUNTED...
A MESSENGER GOES GALLOPING OFF, AND THE HEAD OF THE C.B.C.*, WHO WAS REALLY UP THE POLE, AT LAST ANNOUNCES THE FINDINGS OF THE GALLOP POLL.
CALIPH HAROUN AL PLASSID: 100%. ABSTENTIONS: 0% SPOILED PAPERS: 0%
*CALIPHATE BROADCASTING COMPANY
ONCE THE OFFICIAL RESULTS—CONFIRMING THOSE OF THE OPINION POLLS—ARE ANNOUNCED, THE GOOD PEOPLE OF BAGHDAD, WHO TAKE NO INTEREST IN THE PROCEEDINGS, GO HOME.
NOW, ON THE DAY WHEN OUR STORY BEGINS, IT WAS THE EVE OF AN ELECTION, AND THE WICKED GRAND VIZIER WAS GLUM.
OH, IF ONLY I COULD BE CALIPH INSTEAD OF THE CALIPH!
DO STOP BROODING OVER THE ELECTION, MASTER!
IF ONLY THE CALIPH WOULD VOTE FOR ME TOMORROW... BUT HOW CAN I PERSUADE HIM TO?
WHY NOT WATCH THE SHOW, MASTER? IT WILL TAKE YOUR MIND OFF THE SUBJECT.
... AND FOLLOWING THE FAKIR BELLILAHF (GIVE HIM A BIG HAND!), WE PRESENT THE MAGICIAN DJUGGLAH!
NOT WORTH THE EFFORT FOR AN AUDIENCE LIKE THIS...
... AND I WAS WORKING MY GUTS OUT FOR THEM TOO!
I WILL NOW PERSUADE THIS RABBIT THAT IT'S A CHICKEN!
ABRACADABRA!

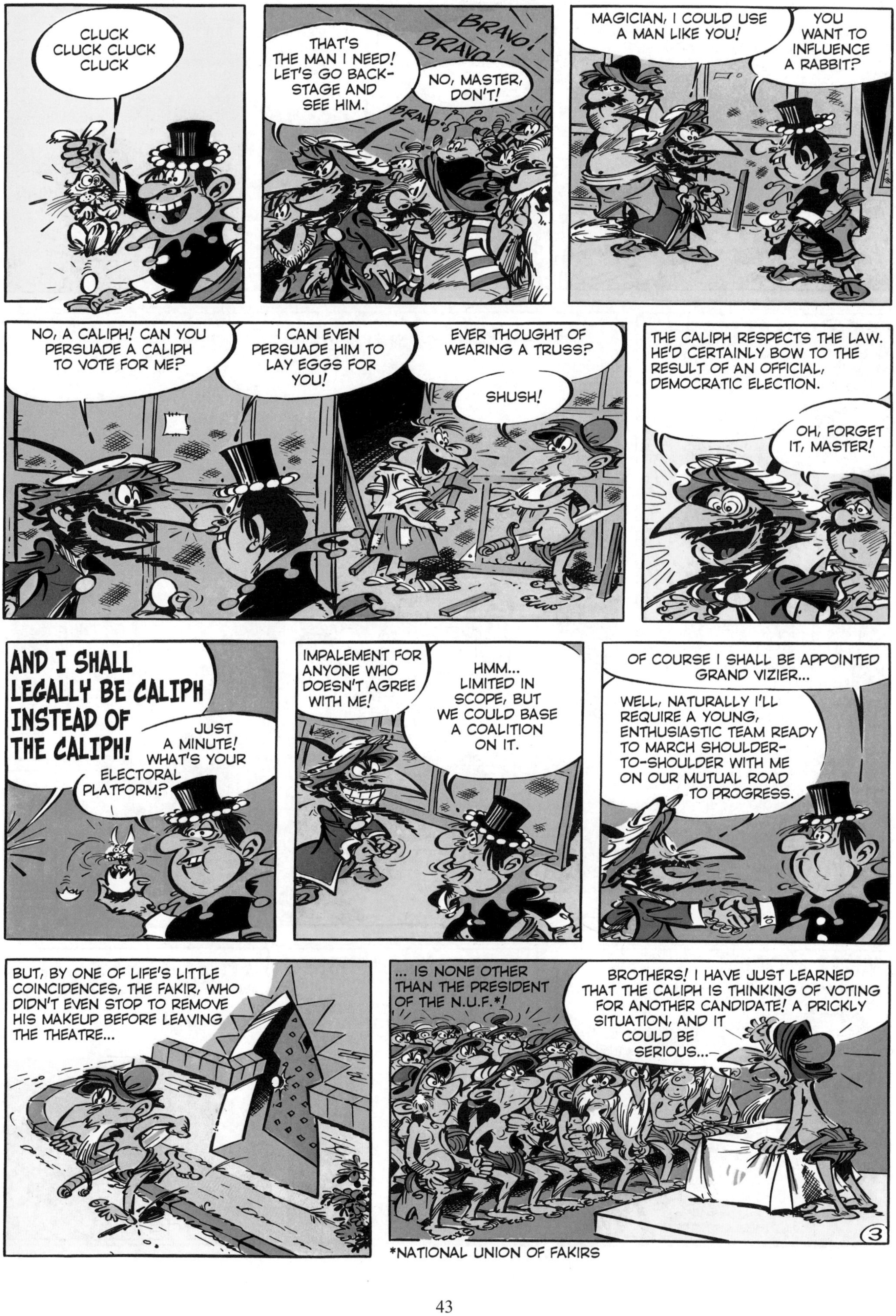
CLUCK CLUCK CLUCK CLUCK
THAT'S THE MAN I NEED! LET'S GO BACK-STAGE AND SEE HIM.
BRAVO! BRAVO!
NO, MASTER, DON'T!
BRAVO
MAGICIAN, I COULD USE A MAN LIKE YOU!
YOU WANT TO INFLUENCE A RABBIT?
NO, A CALIPH! CAN YOU PERSUADE A CALIPH TO VOTE FOR ME?
I CAN EVEN PERSUADE HIM TO LAY EGGS FOR YOU!
EVER THOUGHT OF WEARING A TRUSS?
SHUSH!
THE CALIPH RESPECTS THE LAW. HE'D CERTAINLY BOW TO THE RESULT OF AN OFFICIAL, DEMOCRATIC ELECTION.
OH, FORGET IT, MASTER!
AND I SHALL LEGALLY BE CALIPH INSTEAD OF THE CALIPH!
JUST A MINUTE! WHAT'S YOUR ELECTORAL PLATFORM?
IMPALEMENT FOR ANYONE WHO DOESN'T AGREE WITH ME!
HMM... LIMITED IN SCOPE, BUT WE COULD BASE A COALITION ON IT.
OF COURSE I SHALL BE APPOINTED GRAND VIZIER...
WELL, NATURALLY I'LL REQUIRE A YOUNG, ENTHUSIASTIC TEAM READY TO MARCH SHOULDER-TO-SHOULDER WITH ME ON OUR MUTUAL ROAD TO PROGRESS.
BUT, BY ONE OF LIFE'S LITTLE COINCIDENCES, THE FAKIR, WHO DIDN'T EVEN STOP TO REMOVE HIS MAKEUP BEFORE LEAVING THE THEATRE...
... IS NONE OTHER THAN THE PRESIDENT OF THE N.U.F.*!
BROTHERS! I HAVE JUST LEARNED THAT THE CALIPH IS THINKING OF VOTING FOR ANOTHER CANDIDATE! A PRICKLY SITUATION, AND IT COULD BE SERIOUS...
3

*NATIONAL UNION OF FAKIRS

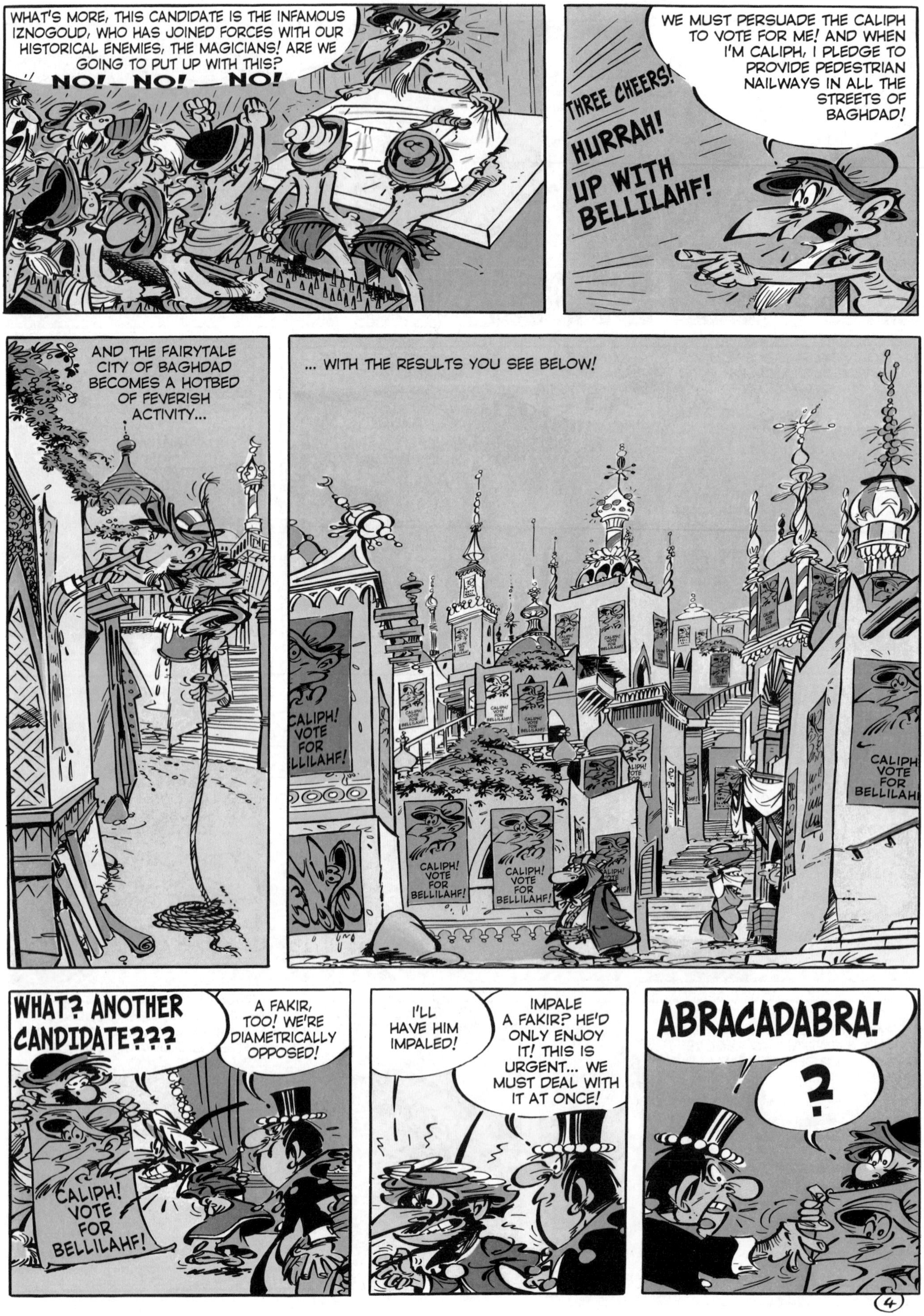
WHAT'S MORE, THIS CANDIDATE IS THE INFAMOUS IZNOGOUD, WHO HAS JOINED FORCES WITH OUR HISTORICAL ENEMIES, THE MAGICIANS! ARE WE GOING TO PUT UP WITH THIS?
NO! – NO! – NO!
THREE CHEERS!
HURRAH!
UP WITH BELLILAHF!
WE MUST PERSUADE THE CALIPH TO VOTE FOR ME! AND WHEN I'M CALIPH, I PLEDGE TO PROVIDE PEDESTRIAN NAILWAYS IN ALL THE STREETS OF BAGHDAD!
AND THE FAIRYTALE CITY OF BAGHDAD BECOMES A HOTBED OF FEVERISH ACTIVITY...
... WITH THE RESULTS YOU SEE BELOW!
CALIPH! VOTE FOR BELLILAHF!
CALIPH! VOTE FOR BELLILAHF!
CALIPH! VOTE FOR BELLILAHF!
CALIPH! VOTE FOR BELLILAHF!
WHAT? ANOTHER CANDIDATE???
A FAKIR, TOO! WE'RE DIAMETRICALLY OPPOSED!
CALIPH! VOTE FOR BELLILAHF!
I'LL HAVE HIM IMPALED!
IMPALE A FAKIR? HE'D ONLY ENJOY IT! THIS IS URGENT... WE MUST DEAL WITH IT AT ONCE!
ABRACADABRA!
?
4

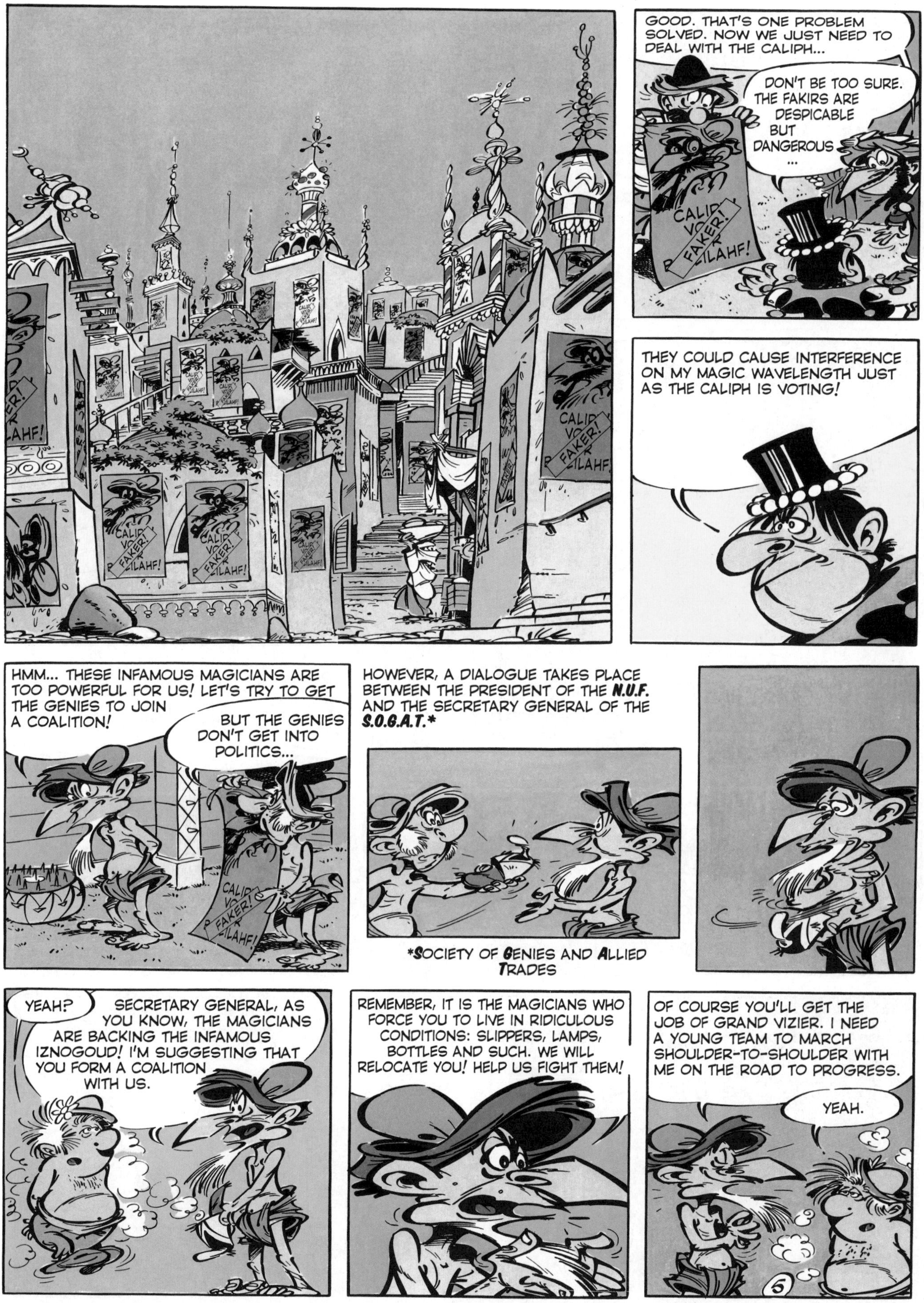

CALIF VOTE FAKER! FOR WILAHF!
GOOD. THAT'S ONE PROBLEM SOLVED. NOW WE JUST NEED TO DEAL WITH THE CALIPH...
DON'T BE TOO SURE. THE FAKIRS ARE DESPICABLE BUT DANGEROUS ...
THEY COULD CAUSE INTERFERENCE ON MY MAGIC WAVELENGTH JUST AS THE CALIPH IS VOTING!
HMM... THESE INFAMOUS MAGICIANS ARE TOO POWERFUL FOR US! LET'S TRY TO GET THE GENIES TO JOIN A COALITION!
BUT THE GENIES DON'T GET INTO POLITICS...
HOWEVER, A DIALOGUE TAKES PLACE BETWEEN THE PRESIDENT OF THE ***N.U.F.*** AND THE SECRETARY GENERAL OF THE ***S.O.G.A.T.****
*SOCIETY OF GENIES AND ALLIED TRADES
YEAH?
SECRETARY GENERAL, AS YOU KNOW, THE MAGICIANS ARE BACKING THE INFAMOUS IZNOGOUD! I'M SUGGESTING THAT YOU FORM A COALITION WITH US.
REMEMBER, IT IS THE MAGICIANS WHO FORCE YOU TO LIVE IN RIDICULOUS CONDITIONS: SLIPPERS, LAMPS, BOTTLES AND SUCH. WE WILL RELOCATE YOU! HELP US FIGHT THEM!
OF COURSE YOU'LL GET THE JOB OF GRAND VIZIER. I NEED A YOUNG TEAM TO MARCH SHOULDER-TO-SHOULDER WITH ME ON THE ROAD TO PROGRESS.
YEAH.

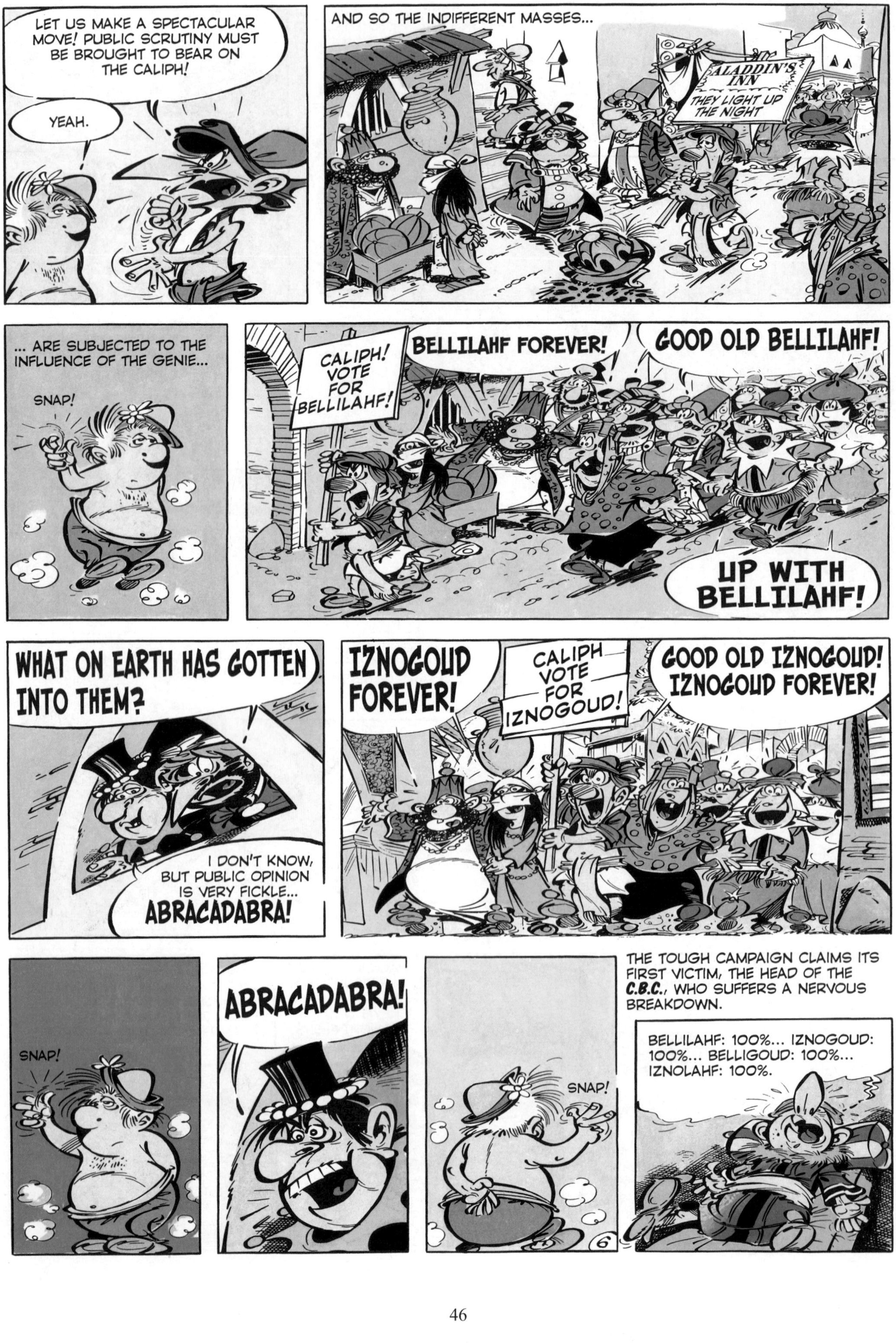
LET US MAKE A SPECTACULAR MOVE! PUBLIC SCRUTINY MUST BE BROUGHT TO BEAR ON THE CALIPH!
YEAH.
AND SO THE INDIFFERENT MASSES...
ALADDIN'S INN
THEY LIGHT UP THE NIGHT
... ARE SUBJECTED TO THE INFLUENCE OF THE GENIE...
SNAP!
CALIPH! VOTE FOR BELLILAHF!
BELLILAHF FOREVER!
GOOD OLD BELLILAHF!
UP WITH BELLILAHF!
WHAT ON EARTH HAS GOTTEN INTO THEM?
I DON'T KNOW, BUT PUBLIC OPINION IS VERY FICKLE... ABRACADABRA!
IZNOGOUD FOREVER!
CALIPH VOTE FOR IZNOGOUD!
GOOD OLD IZNOGOUD! IZNOGOUD FOREVER!
SNAP!
ABRACADABRA!
SNAP!
THE TOUGH CAMPAIGN CLAIMS ITS FIRST VICTIM, THE HEAD OF THE C.B.C., WHO SUFFERS A NERVOUS BREAKDOWN.
BELLILAHF: 100%... IZNOGOUD: 100%... BELLIGOUD: 100%... IZNOLAHF: 100%.
6

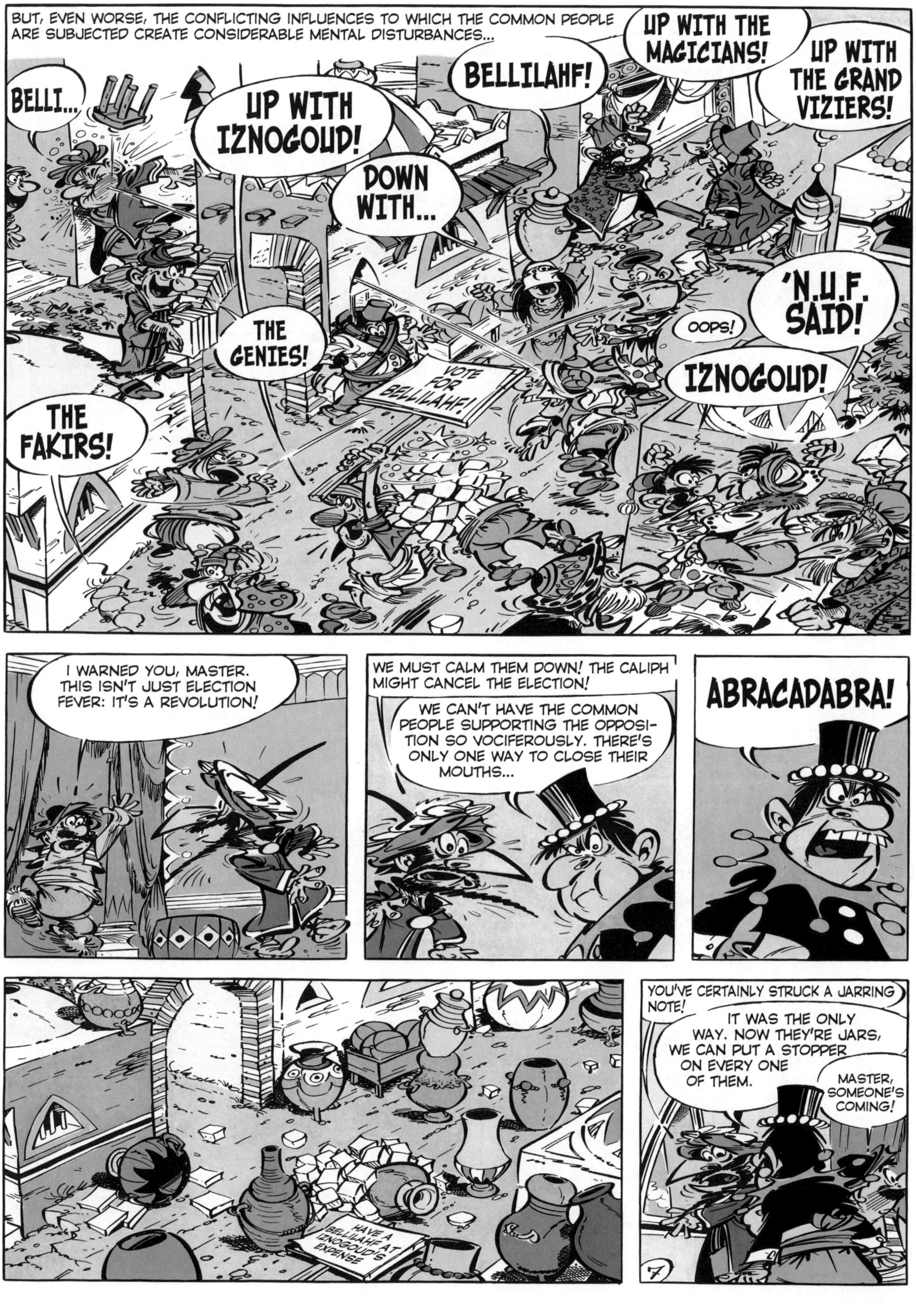
BUT, EVEN WORSE, THE CONFLICTING INFLUENCES TO WHICH THE COMMON PEOPLE ARE SUBJECTED CREATE CONSIDERABLE MENTAL DISTURBANCES...
BELLI...
UP WITH IZNOGOUD!
BELLILAHF!
UP WITH THE MAGICIANS!
UP WITH THE GRAND VIZIERS!
DOWN WITH...
THE GENIES!
VOTE FOR BELLILAHF!
OOPS!
'N.U.F. SAID!
IZNOGOUD!
THE FAKIRS!
I WARNED YOU, MASTER. THIS ISN'T JUST ELECTION FEVER: IT'S A REVOLUTION!
WE MUST CALM THEM DOWN! THE CALIPH MIGHT CANCEL THE ELECTION!
WE CAN'T HAVE THE COMMON PEOPLE SUPPORTING THE OPPOSITION SO VOCIFEROUSLY. THERE'S ONLY ONE WAY TO CLOSE THEIR MOUTHS...
ABRACADABRA!
HAVE A BELLILAHF AT IZNOGOUD'S EXPENSE
YOU'VE CERTAINLY STRUCK A JARRING NOTE!
IT WAS THE ONLY WAY. NOW THEY'RE JARS, WE CAN PUT A STOPPER ON EVERY ONE OF THEM.
MASTER, SOMEONE'S COMING!
7

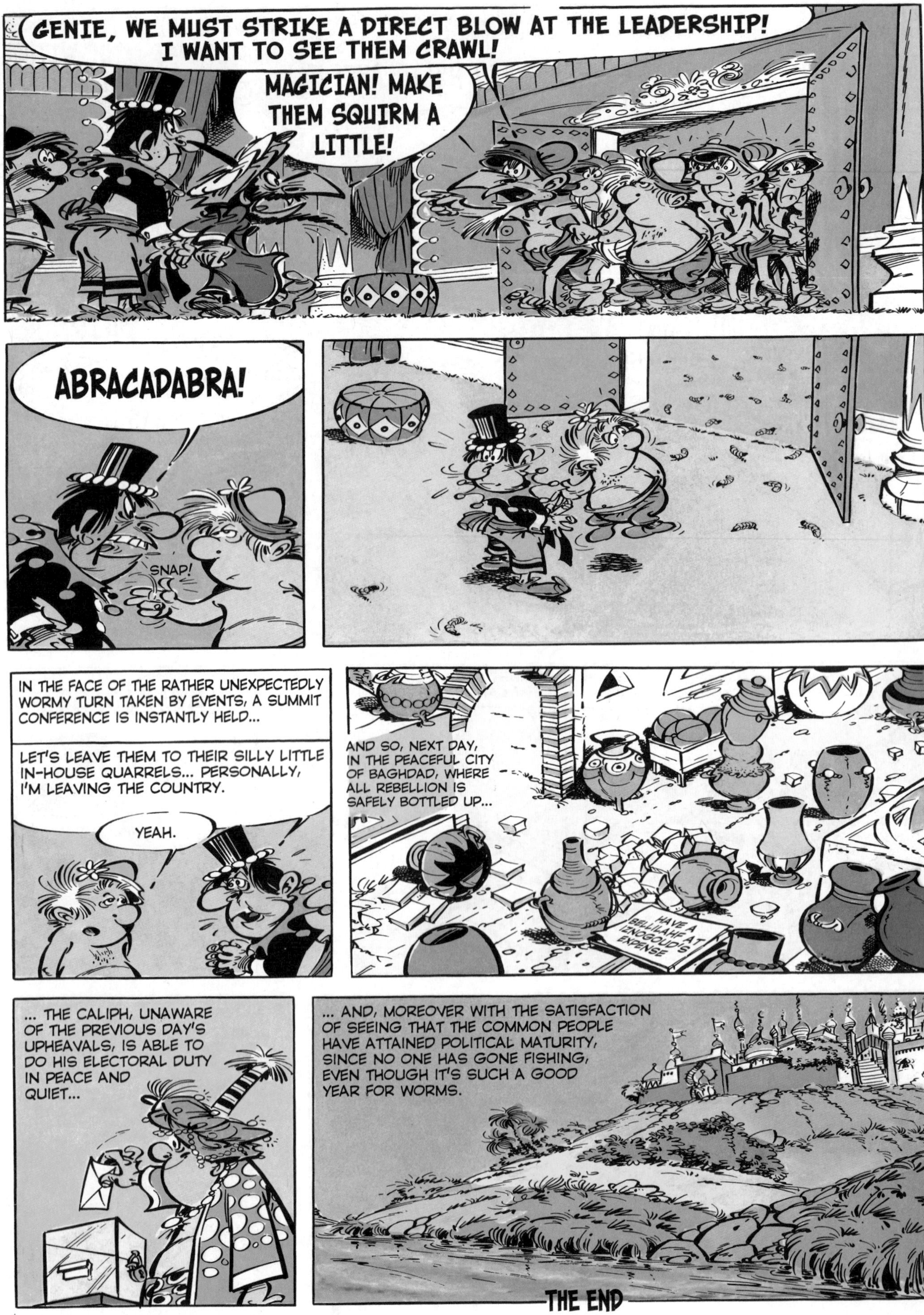
GENIE, WE MUST STRIKE A DIRECT BLOW AT THE LEADERSHIP! I WANT TO SEE THEM CRAWL!
MAGICIAN! MAKE THEM SQUIRM A LITTLE!
ABRACADABRA!
SNAP!
IN THE FACE OF THE RATHER UNEXPECTEDLY WORMY TURN TAKEN BY EVENTS, A SUMMIT CONFERENCE IS INSTANTLY HELD...
LET'S LEAVE THEM TO THEIR SILLY LITTLE IN-HOUSE QUARRELS... PERSONALLY, I'M LEAVING THE COUNTRY.
YEAH.
AND SO, NEXT DAY, IN THE PEACEFUL CITY OF BAGHDAD, WHERE ALL REBELLION IS SAFELY BOTTLED UP...
HAVE A BELLILAHF AT IZNOGOUD'S EXPENSE
... THE CALIPH, UNAWARE OF THE PREVIOUS DAY'S UPHEAVALS, IS ABLE TO DO HIS ELECTORAL DUTY IN PEACE AND QUIET...
... AND, MOREOVER WITH THE SATISFACTION OF SEEING THAT THE COMMON PEOPLE HAVE ATTAINED POLITICAL MATURITY, SINCE NO ONE HAS GONE FISHING, EVEN THOUGH IT'S SUCH A GOOD YEAR FOR WORMS.
THE END